THE RONA DIARIES

The Rona Diaries

One World. Two Pandemics.

Daily Stories and Thoughts
on the Corona and Racism Viruses

by

JEFFREY KASS

Adelaide Books
New York / Lisbon
2020

THE RONA DIARIES
Daily Stories and Thoughts on the Corona and Racism Viruses
By Jeffrey Kass

Copyright © Jeffrey Kass
Cover design © 2020 Adelaide Books

Published by Adelaide Books, New York / Lisbon
adelaidebooks.org
Editor-in-Chief
Stevan V. Nikolic

For any information, please address Adelaide Books
at info@adelaidebooks.org
or write to:
Adelaide Books
244 Fifth Ave. Suite D27
New York, NY, 10001

ISBN: 978-1-953510-69-3

Printed in the United States of America

The coronavirus, otherwise known as COVID-19, which conspiracy wackadoodles incorrectly believe is the nineteenth version of the virus, has turned life as we know it upside down.

The scariest time I can remember before this was when I was a toddler. What seemed out of nowhere, our family was forced to wait in long car lines just to be rationed off a few gallons of gas. The U.S. was in the middle of an oil crisis. But as a little kid, all I knew was there was chaos around me.

Now, all while we're dealing with the worst public health crisis in our lifetime, the other pandemic, which has gone on far too long, has decided to simultaneously rear its ugly head again. Racism. As we sit at home with none of the regular distractions of concerts, plays, sports, happy hours, parties, weddings and nights out, we finally can see more clearly what has been taking place for generations. *Black Lives Matter* is no longer an offensive phrase to many.

This book is a diary of almost daily observations in our now upside-down world during these two pandemics. Corona. Racism. More Corona. More Racism. Like most of my writing, this diary is filled with some comedy, sarcasm, satire, political wrangling, depth, anger, and hope. My goal is to make you laugh, cry, get pissed off, think more deeply, be challenged to create a better world, and even feel happy sometimes. Plus, you're stuck at home most of the time, so you've got nothing better to do than to read more, which is always a good thing.

Just as my family humored our way through the long gas lines of the 70s, I try to insert humor here as well as we navigate these challenges. While many things in life aren't funny, such as death, disease, depression, and economic instability, we can't lose sight of our ability to laugh even in the midst of such unprecedented times.

Rona Day 1: The Toilet Paper Commodity

Who knew there would come a day when toilet paper would be our number one scarce resource? And here we were worried about oil, water and other natural resources drying up some day.

I feel a little guilty that I made fun of my friend Steve because, in 1980, his parents had a bidet. The first time I saw it I had no idea what sick contraption was attached to their toilet seat. I almost was afraid to ask. One never knows what people are up to in the privacy of their own homes. I had a roommate in college who once told me he liked to poop on his girlfriend. Disgusting.

When Steve's mom explained to me that the bidet squirted water up your tush to clean you out, I almost puked. I was only eleven when I learned about this bizarre invention and refused to try it out. No way I wanted anyone squirting anything up that hole. She told me that's how they do it in France so you can imagine I didn't put Paris at the top of my dream places to visit back then.

So, when toilet paper ran out at stores yesterday, even though Corona doesn't cause massive diarrhea or incessant shitting, I had no choice but to rethink my all-out hatred of those mechanical butt squirters. I went on Amazon to research which one would be best for my toilets. I texted my handyman. Was I really going to do this? I had no idea there were so many bidet options.

Fortunately, I scored a Cottonelle twelve-pack at Walgreens a couple hours later, so I paused on ending my butt squirt ban. For the time being.

In the meantime, could y'all please stop buying toilet paper to last the next six months of your lives?

Rona Day 3: Kung Flu

Been seeing nonstop labeling the virus as The Chinese Virus or Kung Flu by Trump and some of his supporters.

Okay, so it originated in China. There's few of us that trust the Chinese government did the right thing when it was discovered. A study published just this week concluded that had China acted three weeks before it did, we could've better contained the spread of COVID-19 by more than ninety-five percent.

It's obviously okay to point those things out. Nothing racist about these facts. Nothing racist about criticizing Chinese authorities. Nothing racist about saying the Chinese government bears some responsibility.

But seriously, pegging it on the billion "Chinese" as an ethnic group or somehow equating Chinese people with the virus? Not cool. Now you've got morons refusing to eat at Chinese restaurants in the U.S. Even a dozen or so people beating up Chinese Americans. It's a virus, not a Chinese virus. Viruses don't have ethnicities.

When George W. Bush was president and some Americans were abusing Muslims here at home after 9/11, President Bush was clear in his admonishment just a week after the horrific attack perpetrated by terrorists from the Middle East: "America counts millions of Muslims amongst our citizens, and Muslims make an incredibly valuable contribution to our country. Muslims are doctors, lawyers, law professors, members of the military, entrepreneurs, shopkeepers, moms and dads. And they need to be treated with respect."

Could you please take a break from your nastiness and do some leading Mr. Trump? We don't need people hit because their parents were born in China.

I think I'll eat some General Tso's chicken tonight just to give him the finger.

Rona Day 5

Day five and panic is starting to set in everywhere you look. People are dropping like flies in Italy. They keep saying it's because they have an older population. But aren't we the second fattest, most out-of-shape country in the world? Are we in for a disaster here in the U.S.?

Japan may sadly lead in suicides, but we for sure lead in carbocide. We consume carbs and sugar in this country like there's no tomorrow. Over one and a half million new diabetes diagnoses a year in the U.S. Thirty-four million people in total. That's ten percent of our population.

My own sugar levels were through the roof just over two years ago. Prediabetic is what my doctor told me. "Cut down on sweets, white rice, and white potatoes" was his advice, but all I needed to hear was the word diabetes and I was determined to do more than eat less cookies, cakes, and doughnuts. I was forty-nine years old and no way I wanted to end up sick for the rest of my life.

I then went four months straight with no added sugar. No cane sugar. No corn syrup. No honey. No apple juice concentrate. No dextrose, fructose, galactose, glucose, lactose, maltose, sucrose. No agave nectar, barley malt, brown rice syrup. The names of sugar are almost endless, but I was determined to learn them all and eliminate them. To rid myself of my love affair with sugar. Thirty-three pounds later and my sugar level is back to normal. I eliminated my addiction so much that today I just stared down the almond croissants in the pastry case as I ordered my coffee this morning and gave them the big F-U!

No way I'm gonna let diabetes *or* Corona take me down.

Rona Day 6

The rest of the world has started going into national lockdown and taking nationwide measures to stop the spread. New Zealand, Australia, Japan, South Korea, just to name a few. For some reason, though, Americans have become so politicized that even science is up for uneducated debate. We aren't just climate experts, we're medical disease experts now. Dr. Anthony Fauci, our lead infectious disease scientist and a doctor who has worked for the last five presidents, is now considered political.

CDC numbers are already considered completely invalid by many. The World Health Organization is now a rogue entity. Physicians are considered the extremists by some.

This unfortunately is why Trump is headed towards failure on Corona. We need a president who's working on uniting us behind stopping the spread of the virus. Not someone who riles people up. Or who treats this as a hoax. All of the presidents since I was in elementary school knew how to lead when the going got tough.

It's bad enough America is becoming dumber by the second, it doesn't help that the leader of the free world is helping speed up that process.

Rona Day 8

I've been working from home for three weeks already. I don't care what our delusional president has been saying. I saw what was happening in Italy and Spain, so I started my shelter-in-place stretch early. No way I wanted the Rona, but mostly, I wanted to stop the spread so people like my seventy-five-year-old and not-in-great-health parents would be okay. And to stop our hospital systems from being overloaded. I mean, I love Italy, but the pizza is still better in New York.

Makes me wish I had installed secret cameras in my parents' house. Oh, the writing and comedy material I would get watching them shelter in place together twenty-four hours a day seven days a week. My parents are basically the Jewish Costanzas. They aren't the best at technology but Corona finally forced them to figure out how to use FaceTime so they can call the grandkids and see their faces. Now that's the only way they call us anymore. Last time they called, Dad proudly told my kids, "We love Facebooking with you!"

Oy vey.

Rona Day 10: 2020 Vision

I had to actually start going to my nearly empty office downtown because there were too many eighty-page documents I needed to read on a larger screen or print out to read. I haven't had great eyesight in years, but now that I passed fifty, it really has taken a turn for the worse. Good thing I have an addiction to funky frames. At least I can be blind and look halfway decent to others with my red, lime green, or blue glasses.

Reminds me when I was first told I had to wear glasses. Third grade. I must've been born vain because there was no way my nine-year-old self was going to ruin my chance with the girls and wear glasses. Mom took me to pick out a pair and every day I would put them on, but as soon as I left the house, I put them in my bag, never to be seen for the rest of the day. I pulled these shenanigans off until eighth grade when Mom told me she had saved enough money to buy me contacts. Seeing in school had become much more difficult, so I agreed to wear them.

Unfortunately, my affair with contacts didn't last long. I couldn't for the life of me figure out how to put them in and would spend sometimes a half an hour cussing up a storm as I struggled to put them in each morning. I'm sure Mom didn't buy me contacts just to listen to my thirteen-year-old self yell "Fuck!" "Damnit!" and "Shit!" each morning before heading to Yorktown Middle School. After a month of frustration, I gave up.

It wasn't until my junior year of college, when I literally was sitting in the front row of three-hundred-person lecture halls just to barely see the chalkboard, that I knew I had to correct my eyesight. Yes, we still had chalkboards back in 1990.

The next day I drove squinty eyed to an optometrist, got a new prescription for my near blindness, and picked out some new frames. I hadn't owned a pair of glasses sine 1979, but I had no choice. I was told it would take another week to get the glasses back, but the good news is I could use frames as another fashion statement. Despite having no money, I always loved funky clothing. Now I could do the same with glasses. I ended up getting three pairs—purple, blue, and red. I remember the day my new glasses arrived. I walked onto campus and I had not seen such brilliant beautiful colors on flowers and trees in years. It was the most beautiful thing I had seen.

Today, my eyeglass collection exceeds thirty pairs, but during Corona, what the hell's the point? It's not like I get to see anyone. I've worn a blue pair for over two weeks straight now. Makes you wonder what really matters in life.

I'm so beyond blind now that I'm just glad bifocals no longer have that line across the middle of the lenses. I'd rather not see than go out of the house with that. Shit, if bifocals looked like that, I'd be down for stay-at-home rules in full force indefinitely. Anyway, now they're called "progressives" instead of bifocals. Sounds cooler than "blind fuck." Yeah! I'm progressive. That's a compliment in my book.

When I arrived at my office building downtown for the first time since I started working from home during this mess, I was a bit apprehensive. Was I putting myself at risk? The security guard in my building, Alex, told me a grand total of sixteen people for the sixty-story building had come to work that day. Turns out, it was probably safer than getting my groceries. Or stopping for five minutes to grab coffee. Maybe even safer than staying home.

Sure enough, of the eighty or so people who work in my downtown law firm, a mere five were in the office that day, spread out over two large floors. I'm at least thankful for the first time being literally called "essential" in life. Who would've thought? An essential lawyer. Has a nice ring to it, no?

The problem with social media is I think we have too much information now. I was feeling comfortable in my sparse office surroundings until I read on someone's Facebook feed that the recirculated air in office buildings could potentially spread Corona and that cleaning crews might leave Corona shit on your desk or other surfaces. Fuck! The last thing I wanted was to get Corona from a surface. If I'm going to get it, at least it should be from being close to humans, which I love. Well, some of them. Damn I miss hugging.

Anyway, since I heard they were still cleaning our offices, I quickly printed out signs to attach to my door that read in large letters "PLEASE DO NOT CLEAN MY OFFICE— POR FAVOR NO LIMPIES MI OFICINA." Alright, calm down, I'm not stereotyping the cleaning crew. They actually speak Spanish, so I was just covering my bases. It's not like I'm the one who called the pandemic in 1918 the Spanish Flu.

The next day, feeling safer, I got to my office and I noticed that my office was spick-and- span and my trash had been emptied. Motherfucker! They didn't even read my sign. Maybe the cleaning crew was from Japan and I needed to add more languages. Okay. New plan. I'll place my trash can outside and close my door. But this time I will make and post even bigger signs. It worked. Office door still shut the next day and trash can empty. Whew. No Corona. And no, I didn't add Japanese to the sign.

Rona Day 11: Stay Home!

Took my weekly trip to Whole Foods to spend $345 on a few apples raised in a good family, cottage cheese from happy mooing cows, and energy bars that cost more than it would to just pay someone to have energy for me. The shelves weren't as empty as they were last week, except the eggs. Only two cartons left this time. At least they were the brown kind. You should try them. Just as good as the white ones if you ask me. Sometimes better.

Unfortunately, Whole Foods was out of unsweetened baking chocolate. My girlfriend and I had planned to make a flourless chocolate torte with no added sugar. It's actually quite amazing how much cooking we've been doing since this infectious mess started. I made duck legs last night and cooked carrots, turnips, celery, and onions in the duck fat. Delicious.

Headed to Natural Grocers, a smaller competitor of Whole Foods. They for sure would have the chocolate we desperately needed. They might be out of spirulina, but no way the organic non-GMO hippies were going to claim the chocolate, too. No such luck. No chocolate there either. But I did score horseradish root needed for the upcoming Passover holiday. Stores had been out for a while, so this second trip in public wasn't a total wasted risk.

I hadn't been to a conventional Cheez-It, Oreos, Doritos–type grocery store in easily over a year. Truthfully, since I took on a healthier lifestyle in 2018, I can count on one hand the number of times I've stepped in a Safeway or Kroger. Not that those stores don't have some healthy things, but walking by color-dyed salmon or factory farm–raised meat disturbs me now. Fake, larger-than-life hormone-fed chicken breasts aren't quite as attractive as other types of fake breasts. I get it. The food is cheaper, and most people can't afford $9 avocados, but I just don't do well in those kinds of places anymore.

For one box of unsweetened baking chocolate, though, why not? I walked into the King Soopers on Leetsdale in

Denver. Day eleven of stay-at-home. The place was packed. Like they were giving out Corona vaccines or something. Or free massages with happy endings. One of the two. I hesitated but decided how bad could it be? As I stepped through the glass sliding doors, I just stood there in shock. Aisles and aisles of people who thought social distancing meant no talking. Hundreds of people just inches from each other. Mostly in silence. No masks. I knew they should've told people that this was supposed to be physical distancing. What the hell is social distancing? Sounds like a psychological syndrome of some sort. We have enough of those.

I hurried through the store like I was in a game show and I had four minutes to score a box of baking chocolate. I ran down the tampon aisle, which had the least amount of people. Finally over to the baking section. No shocker. The minyans of people had wiped the Duncan Hines section out. I heard someone cough. To my left. Another one sneeze. Behind me. I've gotta get the fuck out of here, I thought. This was a Coronafest.

I would've felt safer being sprayed with drugs at Coachella. What the hell was I thinking? I scurried back past the feminine pads and douche and bolted for the door through the vitamin section, which not surprisingly, also had nobody near them. That was 4:05 p.m. Just hours before the holy Jewish Sabbath.

Back home. I sat on my couch wondering if I caught the Rona. My throat felt scratchy for the first time. "Okay, Jeffrey," I started talking to myself out loud. "It takes at least three days to incubate. You wouldn't get symptoms in fifteen minutes." I took a deep breath but made some hot tea anyway, wondering if I would wake up the next morning with a full-on sore throat and the dreaded COVID-19.

I woke up fine.

Rona Day 12: Not All White Bitches Are Bad

The news is reporting someone may have transmitted Corona to a dog.

For almost the first half of my life, I was pretty much afraid of all dogs. But by the time I was in my thirties, I had become a full-on dog lover. So much so that when I once dated someone who refused to hold my hand when I stopped to pet a dog, I actually knew deep down that issue alone meant she wasn't the one for me. Yet there still was one type of canine that scared the shit out of me: pit bulls. So much so that when I picked up Mindy for our first date a year after my divorce, I knew it would be my last the second I arrived.

I met Mindy the old-fashioned way. In the produce section of Wild Oats, an organic grocery store gobbled up by Whole Foods years later. I saw her glance at me a few times before I approached her. It was obvious she just came from yoga or the gym or, who knows, maybe Jazzercise, if that's still around. Her hair was in a ponytail and she was, well, a bit sweaty. But even behind the tousled hair and sweat stains, she was cute. "Ahhh, did you get all dressed up for me?" I joked with her before eventually asking for her number. I wish I could tell you in more detail what else she looked like, but boy do I remember her dog.

Mindy lived in Saint Charles, which was a good thirty minutes from where I lived in St. Louis. I always tried to be a gentleman, so I agreed to pick her up anyway. I got to her apartment a few minutes early, as is unfortunately typical for me. Having listened to my parents argue about my father's lack of punctuality my entire childhood, I have grown into an habitually on-time, or should I say habitually early, arriver. Throw a party. I'll be the first one there.

Mindy rented a red brick townhouse that was connected to other ones on each side. The only parking for nonresidents was along the street, so after I found a space a half a block down, I parked, turned off the car, and headed down the street to ring her doorbell. The second my foot planted on the first step, ferocious barking and growling ensued. I could see it through her curtains, peering from the window adjacent to the front door. A brown pit bull. With teeth you might see in a kid's shark tooth collection. Slobber dripping down the side of one of its massive cheeks. I paused, then took a few steps back down the stairs, then a few more steps back toward my car. Deep breath. I texted Mindy to let her know I was outside, but I didn't think her dog wanted me to come in.

"Oh, don't be silly. Shelly's harmless. We're just excited," she texted back. "Come back to my house."

I know it wasn't the manliest thing I ever said to a woman, not that I'm all that macho anyway, but I couldn't help myself when I responded. "Ok, but I'm not coming inside." Insert smiley emoji at the end to soften the blow.

Anyway. Shelly? Are you fucking kidding me? Who the hell names a killing machine Shelly? Was it short for Sheldon or Michelle? Either way, I wasn't taking my last breath as one of Shelly's human snacks. SHELLY GNAWS JEFFREY. Not a good headline. Not even a good porn title.

I walked back to the now open front door, with Mindy standing there holding Shelly on a metal chain leash. "Are you sure you won't come in?" she prodded me with a charming smile. As much as I wanted to, my fear of pit bulls was just too much. No smile was going to change that. "I'm sorry, bad experience," I (sort of) exaggerated.

Mindy looked disappointed, but honestly, no way I was ever coming back to Mindy's apartment again. It was already decided. This was going to be my last date with her.

I wasn't fibbing about having a bad experience with a pit bull. Besides getting chased by one on my way to Old Orchard Elementary School back in third grade, I had another reason to be scared. My cousin Elana was in high school when her boyfriend's pit bull Bo just decided out of nowhere to take a chunk out of Elana's face while watching TV at his house one night. They'd been dating for almost eighteen months, and at no time prior had the then three-year-old Bo been aggressive toward her or anyone else.

Bo had been adopted at six months old and raised in a good family. He was regularly around kids and had never bitten anyone. He wasn't used to fight. Or trained to hurt. Or hunt. Just a regular white suburban family with a Weber grill and swing set in the backyard. I heard about the story thirdhand since Elana and I only saw each other twice a year or so when my parents took us to visit Toledo to see my Dad's parents. But I've seen the scars that remain across the right side of her face thirty-two years later.

When I moved to Colorado in my early forties, my new next-door neighbors wanted to introduce me to Nicole, who was dubbed as an attractive, smart, and nice Jewish girl who just moved to Denver a few years ago. I immediately looked her up on Facebook to investigate for myself. Let's be honest, sometimes setups don't exactly match up with the description. "Oh, she's beautiful" more often than not means "beautiful on the inside," while leaving out that minor detail.

It's been eight years since the attempted setup, so I don't recall what Nicole's social media pictures looked like anyway. But guess what? I still remember the rest of her Facebook page. Her life passion? Rescuing pit bulls. She literally hosts two to three at a time until they are adopted. Just my fucking luck. There were literally dozens of pit bull photos on her page. There was no sense in asking Nicole on a date where I would get to show off once again how un-masculine I am when I refuse to go inside her house. I wasn't interested in frolicking in the park with three pit bulls after a picnic. I like my face the way it is.

In 2013, the state of Maryland took testimony from experts and determined that pit bulls are inherently dangerous and passed a law that makes owners liable for injuries caused by their furry pit bull puppies. This followed an incident in Nassau County, New York where a pit bull went on an attack spree, injuring a teenage boy and three women over a thirty-minute period. Children's Hospital in Philadelphia released the last five years of records on dog bites. Over sixty percent were from pit bulls or pit bull–rottweiler mixes. Another fifteen-year study from a major American medical journal found that most dog attacks in the state of Kentucky were from pit bulls. And not just attacks, the victims also experienced higher death rates in these instances. The U.S. Army also has prohibited them in many military housing units now.

I've brought up my fear of pit bulls to people who claim to be in the know and they uniformly tell me that pit bulls are not inherently dangerous. That they're not even remotely prone to violence as a matter of biology. It all has to do with how they're raised. And that most pit bulls are trained by aggressive people. It's their environment, they say. I didn't do any scientific research, but I never saw a news article where a poorly raised labradoodle mulled a four-year-old boy because he was too rambunctious with the dog. Or a report of an abused Maltese ripping someone's finger off. Never heard of a French bulldog from a bad home dining on human limbs.

It isn't just pit bull news that causes me concern, though. What about all the news we've had about police brutality against Black people lately, particularly Black men? Really until Kaepernick's controversial kneeling episode, the number of unarmed Black men getting gunned down or beaten by white officers, often caught on iPhone cameras, was staggering. Still insanely high, but did you notice the temporary couple year slight drop in episodes after Colin made us look? I can't imagine what it must be like to live inside brown skin.

I wonder what it would feel like if I was stopped for speeding or yielding at a stop sign and asked to step out of my vehicle just for driving in certain less colorful neighborhoods. Happened to my friend Donovan six times. Let me clarify. Six times in 2019. I wonder what it does to a Black kid's self-esteem when a white teacher calls on white peers in class seventy percent more of the time.

I wonder how it felt when my Black friend Harris told me he had just found an apartment, only to learn upon showing up to fill out his application that he would be declined because, as the middle-aged white man in the front office explained, "Sorry, three people submitted applications first." Keep in mind when Harris originally called two hours prior, he was told there were six available apartments. Maybe the three people each wanted to rent two apartments a piece? You never know.

"All that happened in the last two hours, Tom?" Harris asked sarcastically as he read the man's name badge.

I wonder what it feels like to be followed by a plain-clothed white man in a department store when you just need to buy a shirt. Or what it felt like to my colleague Reggie, a lawyer, who had to leave his driver's license just to look at engagement rings at Macy's for his girlfriend, when I wasn't asked to the do the same thing by the same older white woman after testing the policy an hour later. Now, I personally don't know why anyone with any sense of style would buy an engagement ring at Macy's, but that's for another story. Oh, and they only let him see one ring at a time. For me, she took four or five out at once. Even smiled at me in the process.

I wonder what it must feel like to be seen as violent even when white man after white man shooting up clubs, churches, and the like aren't a catalyst for fear of white men. How it must feel to learn not to carry books into a bookstore, or not carry any bags into any store, for fear of being an assumed thief. It must royally suck to have people look suspiciously at you. "Four years of undergrad and a master's degree, and they still think I'm up to something," my friend Rick reminded me years ago after a horrific traffic stop that resulted in the cops removing his bucket seats to search for drugs that were never to be found.

A 2016 Pew Research study found that college-educated Black people experience far more racism, including racial slurs, than less educated Black people. Go figure. Imagine doing what you can to escape the lazy label imposed on you by white people, only to find out that after years of college, you get it worse. Another more recent study revealed that Black people with Harvard MBAs ten years after grad school made on average $100,000 less per year than their white peers with the same degrees.

I wonder how self-worth is impacted when high school world history classes typically omit a certain entire continent and we're left to the media and movie impressions to learn that Africans are all just one monolithic group of jungle savages. Wonder what it would be like to have my history only be taught in a special short month but excluded from the rest. I wonder what it would be like if my skin color was considered negative or bad luck. Black cats. Black sheep. Black magic. Black curse. The dark side. A black outlook. Blackmail. Blacklisted. Blackened salmon. Oh wait, that last one is okay.

I don't know about you, but I'd be pretty angry or despondent if I had to endure all this negativity and racial hierarchy that invades so many individual and collective minds, subconscious, and space. Let's be truthful, most of us would probably be far angrier, traumatized, or depressed than we'd like to admit. And in case you're wondering, that negative black shit? Most of it only started around the same time Europe decided to lump all Africans in as Black and trade them as slaves. Before that, there was no such thing called "the Black race." Brown people from one part of Africa had no identity with brown folks from a different part. It's true. Look it up. Just in case you're still mad Black folks like to hang with their own.

My favorite white responses of late to Black anger, despair, depression, trauma, protest, and complaint have been pretty consistent. And I'm not talking from KKK types. These are the words from many well-meaning white folks in my life who don't consciously like or dislike people based on their skin color. I recorded them in my writing diary over the past several years.

"I just don't see color," my colleague Lance told me last year. Or my friend Ronnie's girlfriend, Jen. "If African Americans, or whatever they need to be called this year, would stop focusing on race, the problem would probably disappear for the most part." Emily. "I want a colorblind society. Just like Martin Luther King said." John. "There will always be fanatics and racists, but 99% of Americans aren't racist so I wish Black people would stop focusing on race." Bill. "It's racist to give Black people something at the expense of white people. That's reverse racism." David. "Why can't they just work hard like the rest of us and pull themselves up by the bootstraps. Enough blaming already. I didn't own slaves." Brittany. "Of course, everyone should be judged purely based on the content of their character."

My list was much longer.

Anyway, you would never see me caught dead in any boots with straps. Although I was surprised the one time I went to a country bar, Wild Country, just outside of St. Louis. On one of the country band's breaks, the DJ started playing hip hop music. We love our Black culture, don't we?

One seventy-degree day in April 2012, I stopped at a new coffee shop in Denver to do some writing. Don't worry. I don't think it was a story on race, although I can't recall the coffee shop or what I actually sat down to write that day. But I do remember the pit bull I encountered. I was seated outside at a table enjoying the sun when a twenty-something year-old kid tied the leash on his white pit bull to the black metal table three over from mine.

"Stay right here, Lilly," he told her in a high-pitched baby voice like he was talking to a toddler. The owner glanced over at me, probably sensing my apprehension. Maybe he saw the *you've got to be kidding me* look on my face. "Oh, don't worry, Lilly's the friendliest dog you'll ever meet." He then proceeded inside without a care in the world.

I looked over and you know what, Lilly wasn't barking at me. She had one of those doggie smiles that invited me to come play. She was panting in anticipation of a good lick and rub down. So I did the unthinkable. I walked over to her. It was just the two of us. Nobody watching. I pet her. Rubbed her belly and let her lick me. She was pure delight and so happy. I played with her until her owner returned.

"She's really so sweet," I told her owner. Lilly wasn't like all the pit bulls I heard about in stories or in the news. She wasn't like the one that chased me to school in 1978. She hadn't bitten anyone's face off. She hadn't barked violently. Hadn't eaten any teenage fingers lately. But still, can you please cut me some slack and at least try to understand why most of them still scare me? And why lots of other people are scared of them?

Isn't this what we do with people, too. We have a series of really awful experiences and then we develop opinions based on those experiences. So how about cutting Black folks some slack when they express their apprehension about us white folks. What they endure so many days of the year is quite traumatizing.

Rona Day 14: Bats

A lot of articles about bats these days. I never liked bats to be quite honest. They're basically flying rodents. And who likes rodents? I couldn't even understand as a kid why people chose them as pets. Hamsters and guinea pigs grossed me out. If I didn't even like watching hamsters move their fat asses around their hamster treadmills, I certainly wasn't going to take a liking to bats.

To be fair, it's not like I have a lot of experience with them to make an informed opinion. And eating them never crossed my mind, no matter how much of a foodie I am. We didn't have any bats in our neighborhood growing up. Mostly just rednecks parking their Peterbilt cabs on our street and a few Cutlass Supremes on blocks. My only encounter with a bat was in 1991 in college. I lived on a street called Summit just off the Ohio State campus. A piece of shit apartment that cost about four hundred dollars a month. My 1984 Chevy Chevette had its own parking space, but the rest of the small apartment complex was a run-down large piece of concrete. Unfortunately, it's all I could afford.

It wasn't a month into my move there when I woke up one morning with glass shards all over the bed sheets covering me. At first I thought I was waking up from a bad dream. But when I cut my hand on the glass, I knew it was real. I scanned the room. Did someone break in? Was I injured? And then I saw it. The first bullet I ever got to touch. It laid there on the floor next to my bed. The window to the right of my bed had a corresponding bullet-sized hole. I had slept through the whole thing. Of course now, thirty years later, I can't even sleep an entire night just thinking of the havoc Corona is wreaking on the world. My teenage daughter could sleep until noon every day if I let her.

Six months later, I opened the door to my college apartment and something black swooped down near my head. I immediately shut the door. How did a bird just get into my apartment? I slowly cracked the door open again to see if I could get a closer look. I had a clear shot to the American flag hanging on the opposite wall. At the top of the flag was basically an upside-down rat with wings. I closed the door again.

Shit. There's a bat in my apartment. How on earth!

I immediately went to the onsite maintenance guy, Ted, who lived in the apartment complex. Ted was five-foot five. About forty I suppose. Chubby with an unkempt beard. Loved flannel shirts. Ted lived by himself and had been the maintenance guy for over a decade. He always had a Walkman on, and once when I asked him what he was jamming to, he smiled and said "Air Supply."

Ted opened the door to his apartment. "Hey Jeff, what's up?"

"There's a bat in my apartment," I frantically responded.

Ted smiled, as if this was the best action he'd seen in years. "Oh really! Let's go check it out!" Ted couldn't contain himself. "I'll be out in a few minutes," he assured me.

When he emerged from his apartment fifteen minutes later, he was wearing his own version of a hazmat suit. Sweatpants wrapped in duct tape. A puffy winter coat that made him look like the Michelin Man, and a hockey goalie's mask on his head. He was carrying two Wilson wooden tennis rackets. I'm guessing this is the first time he had to use sports equipment in years.

If only iPhones existed back then. The video would've been priceless. The only thing that stopped me from cracking up was I still had a bat in my apartment.

Ted slowly opened my apartment door, spotted the bat in the same place, and before I knew what was happening trapped and killed the bat with the rackets in a split second, not even leaving a drop of blood on my flag or floor.

He exited my apartment with the dead bat in between the rackets.

"There ya go, Jeff," as he showed me the dead bat.

Stunned, I just gave a timid and stammered "th-thanks" and cautiously returned to my apartment, still wondering what crevice the bat had entered through, and still in shock Ted handled the situation like a pro. We could've used Ted in Wuhan.

Rona Day 15: The Rona

Me: Why don't we donate a bunch of your old games and clothes after the Rona is over?

My daughter: Stop calling it "the Rona." You're not cool.

Oh, the joys of being the dad of a teenager.

Rona Day 16: Um, Hello God? Are You There?

I've always had trouble figuring out why bad things happen to good people. Even as a teenager, learning about the Holocaust and the slaughter of six million Jews, I was convinced there was no God. I mean, how on earth could any all-powerful higher being with any good do such a thing. Or, if you're one of those people who doesn't think a deity is in control, how he or she could allow or watch such a thing and stand by. Made no difference to me. Orchestrate or allow it. Neither were okay with me.

The Holocaust affected me so much, probably because that's most of what my Jewish education taught me, that at my tenth grade confirmation at Temple Israel in Columbus, Ohio, I wrote a poem about *man's* creation of God. There simply was no way I was going to accept a God who chose us of all people to be massacred. Hardly makes the concept of *The Chosen People* all that endearing.

Years later while in law school, I started learning about my religion, Judaism, in much more depth, and I slowly started believing in a God. It wasn't that I had answers to the same nagging questions I had as a teenager, but I guess my focus turned to other things. Instead of being obsessed with Nazis and anti-Semitism, my eyes opened to so much greatness and beauty in the world. The miracle of a caterpillar turning into a butterfly. The miracle of the human being. Planet earth. And above all, the miracle of the survival of the Jewish people who had been stomped on so many times, yet still remained alive and strong. Or how Black folks have persevered despite their four hundred years of abuse. I was finally a believer. There was a God running the show after all, I thought.

And yet scattered throughout these miracles, I still struggled. Struggled to find why there was so much injustice in the world. Why Nigerian teenage girls were kidnapped and raped. Why a million plus people were decimated in the Rwandan genocide. Why the mass graves in the Balkans? Why so many unwanted and abandoned kids in the world? Or even on a microscale, why any parent had to lose a child to a disease or accident.

I didn't always let the suffering of the world get in the way of my belief in the Almighty. Instead, I took it as a sign to fulfill my life mission. You always see people who from an early age had an unexplainable passion. Music. Saving the whales. The environment. Writing. Dog rescuing. You name it. Well, I felt as a young teen in the depths of my core that I was meant to fight racial injustices right here in the U.S. I can't explain it. I just knew it was God's plan for me.

And yet, I still struggled. The more I worked on fixing so many systems of injustice, the more sadness I felt. How on earth could a child be born to a mom on crack, I thought, as I tutored at-risk elementary aged kids in St. Louis who had suffered since birth. How on earth could seniors in high school be processed through a school system that left them unable to read or write by age eighteen, I thought as I mentored teenagers. Where was God in all this? The problems seemed insurmountable while this supposed God sat on the sidelines.

Then I got divorced in 1997 and that really hit me hard. Not because I wanted the marriage to work anymore. I had been sad for years. What hit me hard was about my kids. "Why did this have to happen to me," I yelled at God. "Why do my kids have to go through this," I demanded to know. But as was the case with the Holocaust, He was nowhere to be found. It was personal this time, so I decided to divorce God. "I'm done with you!" I shouted.

I flirted with the idea of a god off and on for the next decade or so. Some days it felt plausible. Other days definite. Like when I look into my kids' eyes. Other days absurd. Such as when another calamity hit somewhere or someone in the world. Regardless, I definitely wasn't going to believe in a god that sent Katrina to New Orleans because of "the homosexuals," as several "Christian" evangelical pastors contended. Or extreme rabbis who claimed the Holocaust was punishment for Jews not keeping the laws of the Sabbath. Or extreme Muslim Sheiks who urged people to blow themselves up just to murder Jews, or kill Muslims who weren't strict enough in their eyes.

And now we have Corona. Seriously?

The other day I forced my seventeen-year-old son to listen to Michael Jackson's greatest hits during our workout together. He rolled his eyes but obliged, nonetheless.

"You realize nobody listens to this kind of music today," he smirked.

"Actually, people still will be listening to this when you're my age. But I can guarantee they won't be listening to most of today's top hits," I jabbed back.

He let it go.

I love bonding with him over exercise. He started weight-lifting a couple years ago mostly because I started. It was flattering, and now every time he's at my house he asks to work out with me. He's sweet by nature, but he genuinely likes the time together.

"Heal the world
Make it a better place
For you and for me, and the entire human race
There are people dying
If you care enough for the living
Make a better place for you and for me"

Of all the songs Michael performed, this is in my top three. "Blame It on the Boogie" and "Man in the Mirror" are the other two.

This time listening to the song was different. And not just because I was bench pressing while listening and singing along. Corona made me rethink everything.

I mean look at how clean our planet has been since Corona shut us down.

Venice is once again beautiful.

You can see to the bottom of Lake Michigan.

People in India have a view of the Himalayans for the first time in decades.

Satellite pollution photographs of earth show the clearest sky and atmosphere in a half century.

Air quality in L.A. is at a forty-year best.

Bears in Yellowstone are flourishing like never before because they don't have to avoid us humans in their travel path.

I could go on, but it's clear—pardon the pun—that Corona is cleaning our wonderful planet like never before. At least for now.

But it doesn't stop there.

Parents are spending more time with their kids. Forced to skip a night out with the pals. Or a concert. Or a business trip. And just be with family.

People like me, who are so concerned with clothing, shoes, and vanity, have nowhere to wear their stuff.

So let's see, the planet is cleaner. Parents are present. Priorities are being reexamined. For the first time in years, it's clear as a Corona day to me that this virus is a direct message from God to change our ways. Has it dawned on you why this disease doesn't kill kids the same way it kills adults? Could it be because it's us adults who are screwing up the planet? Who are being bad parents? Who are not fighting for true justice? Who are not fighting for people challenged the most by the system? Who are not making our society a kind one with opportunity for everyone?

I certainly am not suggesting that any person who dies of this is being punished, but maybe as a world we are. And God is telling us to wake the f up and be better humans.

I've been told there will be a new normal when we return to life. But I don't want the new normal to be no touching or handshaking or hugging. I don't want to stop kissing. I don't want the new normal to be masks and six feet conversations. How about a new normal where we act kinder to each other, are better parents, end injustice, and are better stewards of this place called Earth?

Rona Day 17: Don't Sneeze!

Drove to my favorite coffee shop this morning. It's about the only time I leave the house except for my weekly grocery trip and to go on walks or play basketball with my kids behind our garage. The coffee shop Aviano has a strict social distancing line marked with hot pink–colored tape. They take your order behind a large glass garage door then slide your order under a small opening. I think I enjoy just saying hello in person to other human beings these days more than the coffee itself, although it's damn good, too.

On this particular day, I ordered a Kenyan coffee. As I was waiting for my order, I felt a sneeze coming on. Behind me were two other people in line and, off to my right, another couple waiting for their order. All six feet or more apart of course. Most with masks on. The last thing I wanted was for everyone to give me the *oh shit you've got Corona* stare. Before the sneeze was able to make its way out, I contorted my face and fought off the imminent sneeze. As much as I have a problem caring about appearances, I'd rather them think I was a weirdo making bizarre faces before Rona-shaming me.

Even being sort of accused of having the Rona by shamers reminds me when doctors discovered a tumor the size of a tennis ball behind my heart nine years ago. They did a biopsy on it and then handed me a printout of the thirty plus conditions I might have, from ten different types of cancer to HIV. A blood test four days later proved what I instinctively already knew—that I didn't have HIV. But I had horrible thoughts in the interim four days which I found myself begging to have cancer instead of HIV. Turns out I had neither. Some rare benign tumor that was removed, never to be heard of again.

Rona Day 19

The last time I hit the grocery store, it dawned on me that there were plenty of fresh veggies and fruit, yet the snack aisles and frozen French fries were totally wiped out. In related news, today I read that close to twenty-five percent of Southerners who die from the Rona will be under the age of sixty. That's a lot higher than most places. The reason given was because of how unhealthy people they are. Obesity, diabetes, and other diseases are much more rampant in younger populations south of the Mason-Dixon.

As Corona wreaks havoc on the world, and while the planet is the cleanest in fifty years, you'd think this would be the great wake-up call we all needed to treat our bodies and planet differently. Instead, the Kraft Heinz stock my broker suggested I buy some months ago, which to my chagrin had been steadily decreasing, has now climbed steadily since shelter-in-home rules went into effect. Stores can't keep Ore-Ida fries on the shelves, but broccoli, cauliflower, and spinach are available virtually every day.

Speaking of unhealthy, the cotton bandana–masked woman a forced six feet behind me in line at Whole Foods was coughing up a lung the other day. Yes, the phlegm was released into her mask, but still. Either stay the fuck home or at least suck on a lemon Ricola so the rest of us don't know that you're part zombie already. I almost offered to pay for her groceries to be delivered.

Rona Day 20

I went to watch this Netflix show, *Shtisel*, but instead of the next episode popping up when I logged into my account like it normally does, *Tiger King* was on my screen. I had resisted watching the show since I really don't enjoy caged animals and even stopped going to the circus and zoo years ago. But like a bad car accident, I couldn't help myself from taking a look. Joe Exotic. Like Donald Trump had he been born to different parents. My brain has forever been warped thanks to Joe, Carol Baskin, and Bhagavan Antle.

So you guessed it. I binge-watched and finished all the episodes in less than a week. Now I want my seven hours of my life back. One of the less desirable consequences of Corona, I suppose.

Rona Day 21

We decided to go on a hike near Boulder today. Tomorrow it's supposed to snow. Tomorrow is April 12 if you're wondering. Just like Prince warned us on the *Under the Cherry Moon* album. *Sometimes it snows in April, sometimes I feel so bad.* Tomorrow will be a high of twenty-seven and a low of sixteen, so may as well get in a hike now. Guess if you have to be indoors all the time, who really gives a shit? Today the high was going to be seventy, though, and I read that certain trails were still open to people who are not sick so long as they social distance from other hikers. Piece of cake, you might think.

After stopping to get a fresh green juice at a healthy joint in Boulder and downing some cardboard matzah we brought along for the ride, since it is Passover, we headed to the Mount Sanitas Trailhead. It's about an hour hike straight up and another forty-five minutes back down. Not high in the scale of difficult hikes, but the incline was steep and my legs were still sore from a FaceTime workout with my trainer Phil yesterday. If only the snow could've waited one extra day.

You might think that the citizens of Boulder, who are typically on the liberal side of the coin, might appreciate and understand the concept of social distancing. It's not actually a complex idea. Stay six feet the fuck away from everyone you don't live with. There. See how easy that is to articulate? Lo and behold, though, Boulder hikers somehow believe that Corona only infects people who are closer than six feet in front of or behind you. Apparently, the virus cannot move side to side. At least that's what the dozen or so hikers who unsuspectingly passed me on the trail must have thought. "On your left" warnings are not going to scare droplets from your nose from entering mine.

I know I know. Jeffrey, why can't you just stay home like the rest of us?

Listen here. I do stay home. Most days twenty-three and a half hours a day, except for a coffee. Some days I might throw in a scandalous walk in my neighborhood. Or basketball on my own property with my kids. For someone who thrives off human interaction, I'd say I'm doing pretty well with this whole introvert experiment. For now. It's just when I read articles that we'll never go back to the way things were, I want to throw up.

I don't want to go back to the way the world treats our planet. China? India? Venice? You heard me. Take note. I don't want to go back to a world where we forget that it's our family and friends who are most important, not our stuff or working eighty hours a week. But I do want to go back to shaking hands, hugging, kissing, and giving high fives. And doing things. I'll make the vaccine myself if I have to.

Rona Day 21

I was explaining to my kids about advances in artificial intelligence. My kids all know that I only eat organic food and tend to shop at Whole Foods or Natural Grocers. Occasionally even Trader Joe's. Then this:

Me: "Artificial intelligence is going to be everywhere before you know it."

My oldest son: "I guarantee Whole Foods will never use it."

Rona Day 22

Finally figured out why dogs get so excited just to go outside.

Rona Day 26: Y2K

I've never been much of a conspiracy guy. Imagine all the people who would have to be in on something.

The funny thing about conspiracy people is that years and years of believing in this theory or that, they seem to move from one to the next so effortlessly without a thought that their last twelve turned out to be wrong. I'm still waiting on the Y2K world takeover. Or the UN's 1970s alleged environmental plan to take over the world's corporations. My favorite was when Yasser Arafat claimed that Israel was infecting all Palestinians with AIDS to wipe them out. Since then, their population has increased drastically without any AIDS epidemic. So much for that genocide theory.

Man, if I was super wealthy, I'd probably buy a black helicopter and just fly it over a few wackos' houses just to fuck with them. The best part of most conspiracy buffs is they lack even a scintilla of expertise on the subject matter of the alleged conspiracy. All of a sudden, fat white men in their Confederate flag boxers eating bags of corn chips understand how airline fuel and steel work together to explain 9/11. And now, thanks to the internet, they can all congregate and share more bogus information with each other. I miss the days when a neo-Nazi in Arkansas had no way of sharing his warped ideas with a KKK wizard in West Virginia. Speaking of wizards, I never saw a member of the KKK ever do a magic trick, so not sure why they call themselves wizards. Maybe it's the silly-looking pointy white hats. Gotta be. See how easy it is to be a wizard?

It's not that governments and companies are never up to anything bad. We know our government ran a bullshit syphilis experiment on Black men for almost forty years. The Tuskegee Study. They gave syphilis to hundreds of unsuspecting Black folks promising that if they participated, they would get free food, medical exams, and burial insurance. We know that our government incarcerated Japanese Americans during World War II and relocated others to enclosed internment camps. We know our government wire-tapped Martin Luther King, Jr. and Malcolm X.

In the 1990s, we know that an employee of Texaco released secret recordings of executives talking about their anti-Semitic and racist policies and beliefs. Peta has several times provided secretly taped videos of horrible abuse of animals on factory farms. The sugar industry has paid millions and millions of dollars over the last hundred years to quash negative publicity and studies about their wonder crop.

In the 1970s, they even made sure the FDA did not approve an African berry for consumption. It was a four-hundred-dred-year-old sweetener that didn't cause diabetes or weight gain. Synsepalum dulcificum. Otherwise known as the miracle berry. Look it up. It causes your taste buds to think something is sweet when it's not. So cool. Buy some online and have what they call a flavor tripping party.

It's not that we should turn a blind eye to government and company wrongdoing. No doubt it happens all the time. And it's as American as apple pie to question our government. Jefferson and Adams did, although Jefferson was busier screwing slaves. It's American to question authority. Check out the Constitution in case you need a reference point. But we've now reached a place where no evidence is needed for anything, other than your C student high school buddy's post on Facebook to support whatever cockamamie theory you want. But hey, George W. Bush was a C student so what the hell. Good luck making it as far as he did on Cs if you're not of the same ilk. And by ilk I mean white rich guy, in case you're confused.

Corona certainly has brought out today's theories in bulk. We've got people who don't even know what 5G stands for claiming that's why so many people are getting Corona. Forget that COVID-19 is now infecting people in fifty-two African countries, with only two of them with any 5G technology. We've got prediabetics downing Twinkies while they ponder how 5G might be fucking with our immune systems. People drinking high fructose corn syrup like it's Superman potion demanding our government own up about 5G. People proudly claiming they prefer Mexican Coke over U.S. Coke because it's pure cane sugar, as if now that means we're okay.

I get it. Mexican Coke tastes better. But hello people. If you're really concerned about your health the way you claim, put down your 5G glasses for five minutes and do what you can in your own backyard. You gulp down poison every day.

We are the second fattest country in the world. Mexico is first for all you Coke fans. Over twenty-six million U.S. citizens have been diagnosed with diabetes. They suspect another eight million have it but have not sought medical care for a diagnosis. But hey, let's drink the Kool-Aid, literally and figuratively, rather than look in our own backyards.

If I were going to start up some new conspiracy theories on Corona, I'd probably skip 5G and posit that Corona was a ploy by Facebook and Instagram to move our entire society to social media. We no longer need actual human interaction. We can just live through posts from now on. We no longer need to do our hair or nails. To think about what we say before it comes out. We can just play with some picture filters to make us look good online. "You don't look fifty-one, Jeffrey." My favorite comment to some good Ludwig filter I used on Instagram. In all seriousness, I could easily pass for forty-eight without filters.

Or how about this for a theory? The fucking introverts have taken over the world and finally put the clamp down on large gatherings. It's a devious plan to turn the entire world into introverts. I originally thought I'd be okay with this, since I've become way less extroverted than I was even ten years ago. I used to love large gatherings and parties, but now I'm known to ghost once I've made an appearance. I've come to despise small talk and prefer smaller groups with real interaction. But damn, introverts, you've taken this shit too far. I realized I need that human interaction after all. April fools extroverts. Okay, you got us. Now can we get back to the world?

And once you've taken care of your health, come see me about 5G. Until then, it's the O.G., Jeffrey K, saying peace out.

Rona Day 27

Damn, I miss humans. Well, most of them.

I mean not terrorists, or racists, or other kids of bigots. Not narcissists. Not mean or rude people, or the ones that don't tip their waiters well. I don't miss ex-girlfriends who were unkind, insulting, or abusive. Or the assholes who painted a swastika on my door in college. Or their Nazi or KKK pals. I mean, I don't miss televangelists. Or cult leaders. I'm okay not having to see people who have done me wrong. I don't at all miss political campaigners. Or religionists knocking at my door. I really don't miss litterers, or the people who drive cars that spit dark gray smoke into the air. Or people who puff smoke from their mouths into my face. I don't miss people who cut me off on the freeway. Not missing people calling my phone trying to sell me health insurance. I don't miss extremists. I don't miss "friends" who only call me when they need something.

But other than that, I miss humans. Mostly.

Rona Day 28

Pretty sure my clothes and shoes think I was murdered.

Turns out that shit wasn't as important as I thought. And yet I still have one more package from Neiman's arriving tomorrow. I'm a slow learner. Cut me some slack.

Rona Day 29: Civil Rights Activism

Oh, here we go. The protests of government shelter-at-home rules. You've got to be effing kidding me. Masses of people convening on statehouses across the country. In Missouri. Colorado. New Jersey. Minnesota. Michigan. Okay, well the last one, I'd protest just for having to live there anyway. I'm a Buckeye and can't stand that place. The only way Michigan escapes another loss to Ohio State this year is if the season is canceled. Bet you didn't think of that when you protested Corona closings up there. Suckers.

Listen up, science and constitutional professed expert protestors. This isn't Nazi Germany, although the gross irony is there was a protestor in Ohio accusing shelter-at-home rules of being like Nazi Germany while displaying a sign saying the real virus was the Jews. I know. I had the same thought. Dumbass. I never even thought that my cough back in January might've been a Jew cough. Go figure.

Here's the thing in case you missed the difference between these state government rules and the Nazis. The Nazis were doing everything they could to kill people. States are doing what they can to save people. Get it. One, kill. The other, save.

Now that we got that one out of the way, what really irritates me is that we live in a country that had hundreds of years of slavery, but ask someone to stay home for a couple months, and the resentment about some deep freedom being taken away is, well, a bit puzzling. If I were a betting man, which I'm not, I'm guessing none of the people protesting these safety measures in Jefferson City, Missouri were at the forefront of fighting against Black men being pulled over in St. Louis for just being darker skinned. Did that reduction in freedom bother you? Or is it only when white folks have freedom challenged? Don't even get me started on the killing of unarmed Black men by government-trained cops. That lack of freedom ever bother you?

Shit. I'd rather be in lockdown than lockup.

While we're at it, brown-skinned citizens in Detroit were fined a thousand dollars this week for going to a closed park; but let's see, a bunch of assault weapon–toting white guys, a few with Confederate flags, congregate on the Michigan capitol steps without masks or distancing and there are no fines. No tear-gassing. Nothing. Ah, the privilege.

And let me get this straight, protestors. It's okay to control a woman's body by telling her she can't get an abortion, but we can't "control" your body by telling you to stay at home and social distance until this is safe? I'm so confused. Are you pro body choice or not? See, here's the thing, when you congregate closely with others in a protest in the middle of this pandemic, you risk spreading the disease and killing, not a fetus, but an actual walking, living, breathing grandparent, parent, uncle, aunt, sister, niece, nephew, brother, son, or daughter. And this whole time I thought the sanctity of life was of paramount importance to you. Is it or isn't it? At least that's what you said when you supported candidates who want to outlaw abortions.

Now don't attaboy me yet, my dear liberal friends. I'm not an actual fan of abortions. I don't talk about it much because the issue is so loaded with fire that most people close their ears when the other side has anything to say. I was conceived in 1969 (April 1, in all likelihood) when abortion was illegal in Ohio. My parents had no money, no home, and weren't married. As a result, they got married and I was born. It wasn't lost on me years later that if abortion had been freely available, I might've been one of the almost million babies in America that are aborted each year.

Imagine if Martin Luther King, Jr. was aborted. Or Abraham Lincoln or George Washington. Or Moses. Or Harriett Tubman. Or Obama. Or hey, Christians, what about

Jesus? Try this one on for size: Imagine if YOU were aborted. Wouldn't that just fucking suck? Now I'm not advocating that we put women and doctors in jail or suggesting abortion is somehow an easy decision for many people. I'm not here to say that a woman who gets an abortion is evil. That would be absurd to suggest that. I know several amazing people who have had abortions. I'm not even saying that it be considered a crime. It's a very complex issue.

But maybe you could take off your political lenses for a second and think about this idea. We could take the many hundreds of millions we spend on the abortion debate and instead make sure women have the proper health care they need to carry a child and give birth. To have better adoption options and systems in place. To make sure we have enough safety nets to care for the less fortunate in this country when they have a baby. To make sure proper childcare and education are available to mothers. Proper counseling for the decision. What's so controversial about reducing the number of abortions if we care enough for the living? No Michael Jackson reference intended. And what's so controversial about following some stay-at-home rules for the safety of humankind for a bit?

The good ole sanctity of life.

Rona Day 29: Pork Juice

Gourmet cooking is one of my favorite hobbies and thanks to Corona, I've been creating dishes nonstop this past month.

In 1997, I was what is called an Orthodox Jew. What that essentially meant was that I only cooked and ate kosher food; and from Friday sundown through Saturday nightfall, I wasn't allowed to drive, watch television, talk on the phone, or do much else other than eat, pray, read, and eat more. The Jewish Sabbath, or *Shabbat* as it's called in Hebrew.

Truthfully, other than the weight gain from consuming obscene quantities of unhealthy foods each Shabbat, being religious wasn't all that bad. I knew no matter what that about twenty-five hours a week I was off limits to the hustle and bustle of the world. I could reconnect with family, friends, and my community. I could take naps. I could play with my young children and nobody could interfere. The only real exception to keeping the absurdly high number of Shabbat rules was to save someone's life and, fortunately, my law practice usually didn't involve anything more than businesses fighting over money.

Keeping kosher was the more challenging part of being an observant Jew. It meant no pork, no shellfish, and no mixing meat and dairy in the same meal. On top of that, it meant not eating at any restaurants not overseen by proper kosher authorities to ensure compliance with all the many kosher laws. My home then, St. Louis, didn't have any kosher restaurants that lasted more than a few months, so I wasn't able to grab lunch or dinner with friends. No steakhouses. No sushi joints. Not even a kosher vegan restaurant. I wasn't able to just stop and pick up a snack whenever I felt like it. No cheat days for McDonald's fries. Or a five pack of burgers at White Castle.

We kept strict kosher and the closest I ever got to violating the rules was ordering a fresh fruit plate at a place called the Noonday Club, so at least I could entertain clients in my young law practice. The Noonday Club was a mostly (and previously all) white-male, private lunch club in the same building as my law firm in The Metropolitan building in downtown St. Louis. I always felt dirty when I went there. One step below a

Klan meeting if you ask me. It was the only nice place nearby I could order fruit though.

Of course, fruit is already kosher by nature, but the strictest of adherents would still avoid it just in case the knife that sliced the kumquats was just dipped in a jar of pork juice. I'm sure the waiters at this lunch club thought I was a world-class weirdo ordering cantaloupe, pineapple, and strawberries for lunch once or twice a week. Oh, how I would've loved to be a fly on the wall in the kitchen. "That freak Mr. Kass is here again. Who the fuck eats fruit at every meal?" At least most Muslims keeping halal could eat vegetarian in a restaurant. Not Orthodox Jews though.

I'd be lying if there weren't a few moments I almost broke. Mostly foods I craved from my teenage years in Columbus. Rubino's or Donatos pizza with their cracker-thin crust pizzas with extra crispy pepperoni. The delectable Reuben at Katzinger's Deli. The fried bologna at Jack's. Oh, and the obscene one-pound burger at Thurman's Café with steak fries that were easily eight inches long. I only was briefly tempted when I drove my kids to Columbus to visit my parents each year. The rest of the time, I guess I did okay.

Not exactly sure why, but even after I left the Orthodox world in 2006, I continued to avoid pork and shellfish. That was until I was invited to an exclusive private party where some trust fund rich guy flew in a famous New York chef to cook dinner. There were only six of us waiting with bated breath for the culinary delights that awaited us. I was only invited because a client of mine knew the rich guy and his girlfriend's friend needed a date. Otherwise no way I, a random Jewish guy from a lower middle-class neighborhood in Ohio, would've been their first choice.

The first course at dinner couldn't have been worse for me. Pan-seared scallops. I recall loving scallops before I gave up shellfish, but I hadn't had any since my second year of law school fourteen years prior. What was I going to do? Make a scene by refusing to eat the first course served by a celebrity chef who was paid thousands to fly all the way to St. Louis? "Hey guys, sorry, not only am I out of place as the lone non-wasp, I'm a troublemaking Jew!"

I savored the first bite while simultaneously begging God not to strike me down with Zeus-sized lightning bolts. I know the Catholics think they have a monopoly on guilt, but trust me, us Jews aren't far behind. Not gonna lie though, the scallops were absurdly delicious. The only other two times I had shellfish in the over decade plus since were once in San Francisco at a posh restaurant serving, you guessed it, scallops; and the other when my Muslim friend Adnan, who doesn't eat pork, was mockingly gulping down crab legs with extra "Mmmms… this is so good" in front of me. I caved and ordered some. The fancy scallops in San Fran did nothing for me that time and almost served as a final "get it out of my system" finish to my flirtation with shellfish. The crab legs? Well, they were quite tasty, but not enough to completely unwind my Orthodox training. Back to halibut and cod I went.

The odd thing when I was Orthodox is that it wasn't Christians or Muslims who had a problem with my food choices and Sabbath observance. They were quite intrigued and accepting. It was the non-Orthodox Jews who couldn't handle it. Probably fear of the unknown world of Orthodoxy and part the undeniable implied judgment the Orthodox placed on their sinning brothers and sisters. Non-Orthodox Jews inherently knew that their yarmulke-wearing co-religionists didn't like that these Jews were not keeping the commandments handed down at Mount Sinai. It didn't help that some of the more extreme Orthodox Jews, especially in Israel, regularly slurred non-Orthodox movements in Judaism.

I remember when a well-known rabbi in Jerusalem blamed the Holocaust on non-Orthodox Jews, essentially saying that God punished the Jews because they didn't keep the Sabbath, making no mention that entire religious communities were also wiped out. Kind of sick if you ask me, and I can understand how that might piss some less-religious Jews off.

When I was in college, I met an Orthodox rabbi for the first time, and he assured me I was not practicing real Judaism as a Reform Jew. Reform Judaism is a liberal stream of Judaism that focused more on social action and less on spiritual and ritual stuff back then. The rabbi's statement nonetheless wasn't the best marketing technique. I never went back to see him again. I'm sure there's also a fair amount of that subconscious Jewish guilt that drives non-religious Jews nuts, too. Every time they have to see an Orthodox yarmulke-wearing Jew doing Jewish things, it only reminds them of their own choices to abstain.

Whatever the reasons, legit or not, many in the non-Orthodox Jewish world didn't exactly have a positive view of these strict adherents. This hadn't become clearer to me than at my first job at a large law firm in 1997. I was a young worker bee at a prestigious law firm in St. Louis, working seventy-five hours most weeks.

In a twist of the divine sense of humor, as the lone Orthodox Jew I was assigned to work on a case involving large corporate hog farms—known today as factory farms. A hundred or so neighbors in the western part of Missouri sued the owners of five large hog confinement facilities that flushed millions of gallons of hog shit into large outdoor lagoons. It wasn't bad enough that eighty thousand hogs were packed like sardines into large, indoor climate-controlled barns, but all of their poop was washed away with high-powered flushing systems and then deposited into what looked like rectangular ponds. The neighbors, some living a hundred yards away and others living miles away, sued over the horrendous smell, insects, health concerns, and groundwater contamination.

At first it was sorta funny. A non-pork-eating Jew representing one of the largest hog farm companies in the world in a case about the smell of nonkosher pig excrement. Oh, and you can't make this shit up, the pork company was owned by a Jewish family. I remember vividly the first time I visited one of the farms, fearful I would vomit on the spot. I never did well with noxious odors and couldn't even handle when a woman wore a strong perfume on a date. I was convinced I would gag at the first sniff of hog shit crawling into my fearful nostrils. I even warned one of my bosses I might not be the best candidate to travel to one of the farms. Imagine how well that would've gone over. A company lawyer throwing up right next to the client.

After we arrived at the company office in Gallatin, Missouri, one of the company's executives, Bill, drove us past the vast Missouri countryside to one of the facilities. Bill was an engineer. Smart. Well spoken. Gentlemanly. After our thirty-minute drive from his office in a trailer, we arrived at the farm. Eight gigantic long barns placed one after the other. One for nursing. Another for weaning piglets. Another to do what they called "finishing the animals." All of which had their massive amounts of poop flushed into the adjacent cesspool. All in all, some eighty thousand hogs were being raised. A small portion of the seventy-five million hogs raised in similar facilities in the U.S. each year, but still a lot of hogs in my book. I once read there are more hogs in Iowa than people.

Surprisingly, I didn't smell anything. We were told that the pig shit lagoons were supposed to do something called anaerobically treat the poop and prevent awful smells from emanating from the lagoons, except maybe a few times a year when they did what they called "burping." I never believed our client when they originally told us. Odorless shit? Please. But now I started wondering if the suing neighbors, one of whom lived almost ten miles away, were lying. They were mostly farmers themselves, some of whom owned pigs right outside their bedroom windows and had their own motives that went beyond smell. Corporate farming was destroying family farmers who couldn't possibly compete on quantity, price, and efficiency. Was this their way of stopping factory farms, since they couldn't legally tell someone how big their company could be?

After arriving at the odorless hog farm, still in a state of bewilderment, we had to enter the actual barns where the tens of thousands of pigs were raised. They required us to shower so we didn't contaminate the hogs. Us shower? *What the fuck?* How about the pigs contaminating me! Then we put on these special bodysuit prisonlike orange uniforms and began our tour of the overcrowded facility.

I hadn't previously felt any compassion for pigs. My orthodox education had me convinced these were the filthiest, most unworthy and unholy animals ever to walk the planet. Honestly, I wasn't even sure why they were allowed on Noah's Ark. I had met some extreme Jewish religious groups that even refused to let their kids play with stuffed toy pigs or read their children "The Three Little Pigs" because they were so bad for us. Thousands of Jewish children completely unaware of Miss Piggy, Babe, Wilbur, or Porky Pig.

Hatred of pigs aside, I was only in one of the barns for five minutes before I found myself holding back tears. All these animals shoved into small caged pens with nowhere to move. Nowhere to go for a walk. Or bathe in the mud. Hogs pushing each other aside to find a small parcel to even sit down. I hadn't yet thought through the environmental claims if poop seeping into the groundwater back in 1997 but one thing was for sure, this was unadulterated animal abuse under any standard.

It wasn't the law practice I signed up for. I was supposed to be a business litigator. You know, go to court over business disputes. People fighting over money. Money that wasn't mine. I never wanted to deal with divorce and lose sleep over whether a child gets to see a parent. Or do criminal law where someone has to go to prison. Or do some medical malpractice involving the wrong leg being amputated. I wanted a peaceful career and keep the justice-fighting for my personal life.

After we changed back into our street clothes, we stopped to get lunch at a local sandwich shop on the way back from the farms. Bill asked if I wanted something to eat but I declined. I had packed a few snacks since I knew kosher food in middle-of-nowhere Missouri wasn't going to be an option. I probably wouldn't have eaten anyway. I was sick to my stomach after witnessing the way those pigs were raised. Bill went to order a ham sandwich of all things, and when he saw there was no price listed, motioned the clerk to the counter.

"Hey, how much for the ham sandwich?"

"$7.99, dear," the seventy-something-year-old silver-haired, stocky woman said from behind the counter.

"Oh, well I was gonna Jew you down in price when I didn't see one listed," Bill quickly responded, laughing without skipping a beat.

Bill actually knew I was Jewish, and he had seemed quite worldly, at least for a small-town guy. He got his engineering degree from Purdue and spent considerable time outside the insularity of northwest Missouri. He was so courteous and professional in our previous interactions, quite respectful of his Jewish lawyer. But then out of nowhere. Bam. *Jew you down*. I'd been a racism fighter since my college days but here I was, a relatively new lawyer, three years into my career and an engineering executive of a client paying over a hundred thousand a month in legal fees just blurted out the very first Jew-you-down comment I had ever heard in the professional world.

What could I do? If I spoke up, I risked alienating a huge client of the firm. If I stayed silent, I would let pass some horrific and insulting anti-Semitic bullshit. Without a family safety net and my strong desire to keep my job and survive, I gulped down my pride and kept my mouth shut. I imagined how hard it must be for other nonwhite groups to keep their mouths shut every time they experience racism. I once asked my friend Rick why he didn't file a complaint when St. Louis area cops had him step out of his vehicle, searched his car, and removed his bucket seats—all for speeding. "The last thing Commerce Bank wants is for one of its account executives to be on the six o'clock news complaining about racism by the cops." He sadly told me what I already knew.

That wasn't the same reaction I had twenty years later at a restaurant in Denver when a friend of a friend, Dan, who didn't know I was Jewish, blurted something similar.

"My girlfriend's family is so cheap I almost thought they were Jewish," Dan said without a care in the world about who might have heard what just came out of his mouth.

"Yeah, we're real fucking cheap," I stared at him. "How about next time you take a drink from the Bernstein-drinking fountain at the Denver Zoo or enjoy the Cohen Auditorium at the Denver Art Museum, you can remind me how damn cheap we are." I hadn't actually been to either venues yet and made up these particular sponsorships, but most Jews I knew were quite generous and it wasn't uncommon to see Jewish philanthropist names in numerous museums, old age homes, and art complexes.

"I didn't know you were Jewish, bro," was all he could muster back as a lame pseudo-apology, as if his not knowing I was Jewish mattered. Believe me, I wasn't his bro.

I guess that's why I've been so "fortunate" to hear white guys spew racist comments about Black folks most of my life. For some reason, people think it's okay so long as the subject of the racist slur isn't in the room. As a white guy, racists feel safe to let it all out in my presence, as I've learned for the past twenty-six years in my law practice. No way my first girlfriend after my divorce would've yelled *fucking nigger* to the woman in a car that just cut us off on the highway if one of my Black friends was in the car. Hell, she wouldn't even yell it with the window down, so I was the only lucky one who heard her. We broke up after that episode.

It might surprise you, but it wasn't Jew-you-down Bill that bothered me the most working on the hog shit lawsuit. It wasn't even the abused pigs. It was my Jewish boss Larry Goldstein. Goldstein was a partner at the firm and had asked me to work on the case when it was filed two years prior. Goldstein wasn't the nicest boss, always yelling at younger associates like me. Assigning absurdly irrelevant research projects just to make sure we had to stay at the office late some nights or work a weekend.

When the three-month trial began to determine if the hog farm corporation had to pay millions to one-hundred and eight of its shit-sniffing neighbors, our legal team was easily in court and at the office a combined sixteen hours a day. We ate dinner at the office every night. That was difficult for me, since I was the lone kosher-keeping Jew at the firm. When I realized dinner would be catered in each night, I introduced a kosher catering company to Goldstein's secretary, Sally, who was tasked with ordering dinner each night. Goldstein wasn't religious and had made offhand disparaging side comments about my religious views for over two years already.

"Jeff," he always called me, despite the fact that I went by Jeffrey, "I think you guys believe in this religious crap just so you don't have to come to the office like the rest of us each Saturday." Goldstein had made this comment a week into working on the hog shit case when he was reminded that I didn't work on the Jewish Sabbath. I didn't respond.

"You know, you religious Jews aren't any better than the fundamentalist Christians," Goldstein randomly quipped one morning as we were about to go over some research I had just finished on nuisance law. Nothing to do with what we were working on. Just decided to try to make me feel like shit that day as he had done so many other days.

"Did you enjoy your *hooooollly* Sabbath," he once sarcastically remarked, emphasizing the word holy in a disparaging way on one of the many Sunday mornings he had young lawyers come to the office, even if there was nothing to do.

I knew given Goldstein's disdain for my type he wasn't going to agree to allow a kosher catering company to prepare our meals, so I had to get creative. I told the kosher caterer to not put any stickers on the packaging that would label the food as kosher. Goldstein wouldn't suspect anything. The catering company wasn't Yankel Lebowitz's Kosher Catering. It was just called Reservations. Goldstein would have no idea. Neither would his assistant Sally.

The first night went off without a hitch. Reservations Catering delivered Caesar salad, eggplant lasagna, and garlic bread to the office at six thirty. Goldstein, who was on the chubbier side, immediately dug in first among the eight lawyers working on the case, filling up his plate with an oversized piece of lasagna and three pieces of garlic bread. He skipped the salad. "Mmmm… this is so good," were the first words out of his mouth after taking a first bite. I just watched him eat with a guilty eye, like I had fed him poison and was waiting for him to keel over in pain.

Over the ensuing month, Goldstein would go on to inhale plates and plates of kosher brisket, spaghetti with meatballs, hoagies, roasted chicken, and other traditional meals. Definitely no matzah ball soup or falafel to cause any concern or raise Goldstein's self-hating Jewish eyebrows.

Then it happened. It was Wednesday, February 3, 1999. We were one month into the trial of listening to family after family take the stand to testify about their life living next to factory hog farms. The day had just ended with a family who testified about all their alleged health problems they claimed were caused by the hog farms. Headaches. Shortness of breath. Blurriness. Vomiting several days a week when they walked outside. I say alleged because we already knew many weren't being truthful.

Reservations Catering had just delivered the nightly dinner. This time, General Tso's chicken and rice with eggrolls. The only difference? The foil pans had stickers plastered all over them. KOSHER. CERTIFIED BY THE VAAD OF HOEIR OF ST. LOUIS. That was the kosher-certifying agency in St. Louis which had given the kosher-okay to Reservations Catering. The stickers were there to let kosher-keeping Jews know that the food was acceptable to consume. But this time, Reservations Catering forgot to leave the stickers off our meal as I had instructed them.

"Who the hell ordered the food this time," Goldstein yelled before I had a chance to remove the labels. "I didn't authorize this! SALLLLYYYYYY!"

I felt bad that his secretary might endure his wrath, even if temporarily until he learned I was behind the clandestine plan.

"Larry, we've been eating this food for a month with no problems. Everyone likes it," I nervously but boldly responded.

"I don't give a shit, Jeff. You're the only one who needs to eat this disgusting crap. I want food from a normal place."

You might think upon reflection by Goldstein, the whole episode would blow over and we'd continue eating as we had, but no such luck. Goldstein immediately informed Sally that she was to choose a new caterer by the next day. Except for Friday night Sabbath dinners, when I wasn't at work, February 3 was the last real dinner I got to eat for the two months left in the rest of the trial. I was relegated to packing my own food which ended up being cold dinners since there was no place to heat up kosher food at the law firm.

The irony about the whole thing is that Goldstein wasn't exactly what you'd call in shape. He was a good forty pounds overweight in his five-foot-six stocky frame. Add in his coke bottle thick glasses and bizarrely side-parted haircut to the mix and this wasn't exactly someone who should've been in the put-others-down business. I would've thought he would have compassion for others' differences since I'm guessing his teenage years weren't exactly spent winning popularity contests. He's a self-described liberal Democrat, too.

That's the dilemma for the modern Jew. We get it from the Jew-you-down white folks, the KKK, the alt-right. And we get it from the self-described caring far left. We even get it from the Goldsteins of the world.

Kumquats and pork juice. What a disgusting combo.

Rona Day 30

I stopped at a coffee shop on my way to pick up my kids from their mom's. Corvus Coffee Roasters in southeast Denver. They are my number three coffee shop in Denver and my go-to when I pick up my kids. Their mom lives on that side of town. My main coffee shops are Aviano, which is only a few minutes' drive from my house, and Little Owl in downtown. I miss the gang at Little Owl, but I rarely go downtown since Corona started. I sometimes go to Unravel, too. They actually don't use paper cups. You pay twenty-five cents for a glass jar and get it back when you return the glass. They even own their own coffee farms in Ethiopia. I love the owners and the vibe there. Ethiopian coffee just isn't my fave, although Ethiopian food is my jam.

At Corvus this morning, I had a nice discussion with barista Trevor about the differences in some of the countries from where their coffee originates. May sound boring to you but I love love love coffee. Made me want to add Bolivia to my travel to-do list. Of course, right now, I'd be happy adding driving anywhere ten minutes from my house to my places to see. I grabbed my Bolivian coffee. "Thanks so much for working, guys," I said as I turned to leave. Trevor's coworker, a very early twenty-something short blonde woman (read kid in my book), Kelsey, clearly craving human interaction, chimed in. "I'm just so glad I get to work here," she said excitedly, almost coaxing me not to leave yet. "I can't handle not talking to people in person. I get to make new friends every day here. It's not my main job. I'm lucky. I still have that one, but we just work from home on a computer. I keep this one so I can actually see people." Her smile hadn't left her face.

I was happy for Kelsey and her positive attitude, but I left Corvus a little depressed. I miss making new friends, too. The two minutes of interaction getting my coffee in the morning is one the main highlights of my day now. Pondered if I should add part-time barista to my list of talents, except I'm not sure I could handle watching people ruin a nice Rwandan or Peruvian coffee with sugars, flavored syrups and the like. You'd never get me to say things like "Would you like cream or sugar?" Ewwww. I'd be more like, "You'll fucking drink this coffee the way it was intended. Straight. Black." Asking to add shit to coffee is like when your kid asks to put ketchup on the gourmet meal you just prepared. My kids know better. Or at least they're polite enough to pretend.

Rona Day 31

Instead of pouring buckets of ice on our heads, why couldn't we just do a "stay at home" challenge and donated to charity? We would've been done with this shit a month ago.

Rona, I forgot which day this is

Lots of people having weird dreams these days.

I went from dreaming I was cooking a live chick that had gigantic black bug eyes in a large soup pot, having it fly out when it got too hot, land next to me and stare me down, to now I'm apparently sleep-rapping. I don't even like that shit. I mean I love rap, but not that incomprehensible shit. Hit it hut it hit it hut it or whatever they're yapping.

One of my teenage kids loves country and rap music. I'm only responsible for half of that. I told him if he combined the two he'd be listening to crap.

Anyway, now you know why I don't take drugs.

Rona Day Whatever: "That's Not Appropriate"

I try not to judge others' actions when I see something that doesn't seem quite right. But sometimes it's hard not to. Today, as I was leaving Aviano after picking up my morning coffee, I had the pleasure of watching a thirty something year old man whack his five year old in the tush. I don't mean a little pat, but a full on spanking. "How many times have I told you," is all I heard as I listened to the cute little kid cry a real cry.

It brought back a college moment for me. When I was pledging a fraternity at Ohio State and my designated "big brother" warned me that I was the lone pledge who was going to be paddled next Tuesday night for getting smart with some of the older brothers, I wasn't at all scared as I had already experienced the belt enough times as a kid. But when my big brother said paddled, what he meant was they take these wide inch thick wooden paddles that are shaped like mini oars and then they hit them squarely across your ass. I think I prefer the belt to be honest.

The difference with this pending beating is I was prepared. I showed up pretending I didn't know what was headed my way. Unbeknownst to my frat punishers, I had padded my underwear with layers and layers of items. A small hand towel covering my ass, and then several more layers of toilet paper stuffed in my underwear on top of the towel. I didn't wear jeans that day since the padding was too noticeable when I tried them on earlier. Instead, I showed up in baggy sweats, which hid my secret protective gear. I was a bit concerned I would be found out since I was always a bit of a fashion snob and I don't think anyone ever saw me in sweats before. I actually had to buy a pair. I went into credit card debt in college so I could at least look nice, however poor I really was.

One of the seniors, Jonathon, who was usually pretty nice, shouted for me to come up to the main room. His tone sounded livid.

"UP HERE NOW!!"

I hadn't heard him speak like that before. A part of me knew it was an act, since nothing we were up to was all that important in the scheme of life, but if it was a show, he certainly pulled off real sounding anger. The windows in the main room, which lined most of the entire length of the house, were all covered in night black sheets. There was a single chair in the middle of the room. And a television with just static playing loudly. Like out of a horror movie, which I never liked. Shit, I think the last time I went to a horror house on Haloween was when I was 14 and I grabbed the girls coat in front of me and hid behind her I was so scared.

I was told to stand a few feet from the empty chair when several members I had barely seen before proceeded to blindfold me. Then the real fun started.

"Put your hands on the chair and bend over," a voice I was not familiar with barked out. "They should've made the K in your last name silent, you fuckin' prick." Little did he know a few years later I would go on to be President Prick of this little unimportant frat of daddy credit card carrying mostly rich suburbanites. A frat I would later resign from, but that's a story for another day.

Then the fury came without any warning. WHACK!!

Someone took a single crack at my ass. Even with the padding, I could feel it was going to leave mark but I did nothing more than produce a faint grunt. When you don't know a hit is coming, your body really isn't ready for the contact and I could feel the force even in my neck and lower back. In retrospect, I should've feigned more pain because my perceived toughness just invited another blow. I always cried when Dad belted me so I should've known to do it again.

WHACK WHACK.

Two more cracks, this time causing my eyes to water a little. Still, the Charmin padding had generally worked. But to avoid further hits, I yelled out a convincing "Owwww! What the fuck!!"

I could smell marijuana and hear in the background that people were drinking during this delightful episode, so I decided to advance my budding acting career before things got out of control. I can't imagine what it would've felt like if I hadn't stuffed my pants.

"My knees. My knees. Fuck. I think I pulled something."

I got up without asking, blindfold still on, and started limping around without going too far. The whisper behind me was clear. "He's learned his lesson." That's when the blindfold came off as twenty or so juniors and seniors just laughed with piss tasting Milwaukee's Best beers in their hands.

I actually wasn't entirely clear why I was getting a beating, but I understood that's just what fraternities do so I never asked. I wouldn't be surprised if I had mouthed off to someone at some point. I wasn't one to take shit and I always had a crass sense of humor to boot, so I'm sure I pissed someone off. Hell,

I've been pissing off certain people for the better part of thirty years since.

I wish had been able to predict when Dad was going to give be the belt. I could've used the old tissue paper in the sweat pants trick back in 3rd grade when I got my first lashing. The truth is, compared to most of my Black friends I met beginning in Middle School, I had it easy. Some of them got it at least once a month. Dad only gave me the belt maybe once a quarter, like a dividend paid out from owning stock, except my family didn't own any stocks so we got the quarterly belt instead. By the time I reached high school, I only got the belt one more time.

I still remember that first time. It was Rosh Hashanah 1978. Dad and Mom had been fighting about money, as they did many times and still do forty years later, although I think it's decreased finally.

"We can't afford to pay damn Temple Israel," Dad yelled, understandably anxious about paying our synagogue dues after receiving a letter threatening to keep us from going to Rosh Hashanah services that year if we didn't bring the account current. In bad judgment, I followed it with some smartass comment from me that obviously hit a nerve with Dad. And that's when I was introduced to the Pierre Cardin belt. Figures the only time my family could afford leather was for belts.

When I became a father to a sweet little boy in 2001, I didn't want to repeat the anger of the past. I was determined not to lay a finger on my kid. I was doing a good job until he was five and had disobeyed me. It wasn't anything serious, but I nonetheless tapped him on the tush. Nothing hard.

"That is not appropriate," my already smart toddler swiftly responded. That's when I cried more than him, and it was the last time I ever spanked any of my three kids. I've mostly exhibited calm behavior in front of my kids so I can inherently teach them to be calm anyway. And the problems that arise are typically dealt with through calm talking. So far so good. Three teenagers in and no heart attacks for me.

Rona Day 34

The viciousness of how people talk to each other online these days is so out of control that in some bizarro world, it's kind of comical. Liberals are called "libtards" because they might espouse a view that people should get universal health care or free education. Anyone who supports Trump, even if their support has nothing to do with race, are called racists. Okay, I get it. It's hard to give a free pass to Trump supporters given Trump's blatant bigotry and verbal abuse, or his comments giving tacit and sometimes overt approval to racist extremist groups. Or his hiring of extremist xenophobes in his administration. Still, our reaction to basically anyone on the other side has gotten absurd. People can't even talk to others with differing views on any issue of importance.

Today I was called a moron and a racist, both by right-wing fanatics. Now, of course, I tend to the liberal side on a good 75% of the issues, and I have struggled with how anyone can continue to support the imbccile in charge, but it did seem a bit ironic this crowd was so concerned about racism for a change.

Rona Day 36: Cancel Culture

The frequency in which we react and react to each other, typically on social media, without any regard for the other, is increasing at alarming rates. I almost can't even comment on any topic, however respectful, without being called some name or labeled unintelligent. And let's not kid ourselves, it comes from the left and right.

Recently, I merely posted on a discussion thread on Facebook that I thought Israel should stop threatening to annex one third of the West Bank when I was immediately pounded with "you're an anti-Israel Jew hater." I decided to delete my comments altogether as this clearly wasn't the forum for honest debate. It was almost comical the language used against me given my background, except I wasn't laughing.

Another moment I had commented that "Trump's leadership on Corona is awful" when I was met with "Libtard! You have TDS!" That's Trump Derangement Syndrome in case you were still wondering.

We've all been the perpetrator or victim of an exchange not dissimilar to one of the scenarios above. Despite my deep love for all humans, including and especially my Arab cousins, I was blasted as anti-Palestinian and pro-genocidal just last week for expressing my dislike of Ilhan Omar's incessant offensive "Jewish money" tweets.

I get it. It's frustrating to see so many people continue to support systems of racism. It gets on our nerves to see so many people rejecting the life experiences of others. It's hard for some us to see people refusing to wear masks despite medical experts. Even harder to understand people supporting Trump when he's said and done so many offensive things. These are emotional issues.

Well-meaning folks opposite of us get irritated when they're called racists because they support Trump despite some of them not consciously feeling anything negative about Black people.

Many of us are faced with the difficult balancing of the real life fight for justice and not remaining silent in the face of oppression, with the usually ignored known fact that systems are harder to change when millions aren't listening to a word we say. Do we even want a society where anything said that falls outside of our sphere of beliefs is immediately demonized?

I'm not suggesting we just ignore offensiveness. Or that we let go things and words we find destructive. Or that we give politicians or celebrities a free pass in the name of conversation. Or that we stop shouting in loud speakers at justified protests. I'm not advocating that we pretend injustice is acceptable. Or that racist or anti-Semitic tweets are totally fine.

Still, we need to do a better job digesting and processing before jumping. We need to do a better job of trying to understand why the person supposedly opposite you feels, thinks or acts the way they do. How did they get to that place? What are their life experiences? It could be someone is not knowledgeable on a topic and they don't even know it. It could be someone suffers, like most of us, from some level of unconscious bias on a topic. Or maybe they don't fully appreciate what offends other communities and why. It could be that a person experienced something traumatic related to the topic. It could be their unconscious thoughts are in control. And yes, it could be the person on the other side has a good idea. Or the opposite--it could be the person is a racist. Or a moron. Or just plain absurd.

If we're going to better society at a faster pace, though, we need to first take a step back and proceed, as one social justice warrior and Urban Leadership of Foundation of Colorado CEO Dr. Ryan Ross once taught me, *with grace*. I recently found myself getting angry with people in my circle who were still supporting systems I saw as racially bankrupt. That's when Dr. Ross stepped in and urged grace. Grace means listening even when it's uncomfortable. It means doing the one thing we ask of others, even when we don't want to--to try to understand where *the other* is coming from. In turn, our more graceful response might just be that much more impactful and a real conversation can start. Typically more effective than "What the fuck are you thinking" responses.

Really, what good do our efforts matter if we're simply having conversations with people who only agree with us, but we yell at or cancel the people who don't.

When Barack Obama was running for the U.S. Senate seat in Illinois in 2004, my dear friend Rick invited me to attend a $100 a person fundraiser to meet this unknown community organizer from Chicago. "I heard he's the real deal," I recall Rick telling me as I responded with my normal skeptical look when it comes to politicians. The event was at the new Westin Hotel in downtown St. Louis. I remember that day well. Obama may have not yet known his fate, but it's the day I knew I had just met our first Black president.

"We have to stop disagreeing with everything the other side has to say just because it's coming from the other side," Illinois State Senator Obama began. "I disagree with George Bush on a whole host of issues, but if he has a good idea, it isn't bad just because it's from George Bush. When he talks about personal responsibility, I agree with him. I disagree with him that the government can't also fill a critical role in helping struggling communities."

Obama may have not been prepared for the onslaught of unprecedented criticism and disagreement that was coming his way when he became president four years later, but his words are needed today more than ever.

Set Trump antics and demon sex alien sperm doctors aside. We need to do a better job of hearing each other. Listening to each other. Understanding each other. And not immediately canceling each other's ideas, thoughts and actions before we digest and respond.

The only remote chance we have of fixing what ails our deteriorating nation, fixing systems of racism, fixing economic disparity and the like, is to return to the days of having real life conversations.

Grace isn't just for meals.

Rona Day 38: Generation Selfish

I just learned that kids in their 20s are hosting underground nightclubs around Denver. And they're posting party pics online to boast their fun. I'm sure it's elsewhere, too. Full on with DJs, dancing, drinks and of course no distancing or masks. It's a bit interesting. The generation who appears to be the most accepting and liberal, and who are the self-described most caring towards fellow human beings in need, seem to completely ignore the impact they could have on their parents and grandparents. Or even a friend with asthma or diabetes. Doesn't seem so caring or liberal to me after all.

I'll take a millennial any day.

Rona Day 39

New York Mayor Bill DeBlasio literally just publicly denounced "the Jewish community" for their failure to follow Corona social-distancing rules. Who is this Jewish community?

I'm not going to pretend that elements within the ultra-Orthodox, mostly Chassidic community in Brooklyn and Israel weren't late to the Rona party. That's why their COVID caseload and death toll has been much higher. I've spent considerable time in those communities. Part of it is the rank and file in those communities are not on Facebook or glued to smart phones. Most have no access to the mainstream media. Most do not even own internet-capable phones or computers. I know that sounds bizarre, but they believe there is way too much unholy stuff on the internet, so it's banned in many of those communities. Unholy stuff on the internet? That might sound endearing, but they also typically ban secular math, science, and reading after age fourteen. Given their insular life, the hysteria about Corona didn't hit them as quickly as other communities.

Add that to their general distrust of nonreligious institutions and there was a perfect storm for a visible minority within those communities to not take Corona seriously. Some still aren't. But for a while now, at least some of their leaders finally have come out forcefully about following the rules. Too many revered rabbis have passed away due to Corona, so you don't need the mayor to tell them, although sadly there still are some who don't get it. Not to mention that same week there were several other groups of people flaunting the distancing rules and Mayor D never called out their collective ethnic identities.

But regardless of whether a thousand of hundreds of thousands stupidly gathered closely together for a funeral, or prayed side by side, there is no collective "Jewish community" to blame. Millions of religious and nonreligious Jews around the world are following the Corona rules just like most people. Imagine if the mayor said that the Black community needed to stop committing crimes. Black folks would be justifiably pissed at such a bigoted and baseless comment.

Racism is precisely when we start group finger-pointing because we see a member of the group do something we find distasteful or wrong.

Ergo, Mayor DeBlasio, you're a fucking racist. Not all mayors. Just you.

Rona Day 41: Random Selection

I've gotten the stinky eye the few times I haven't worn a mask. I wear one most of the time, but it's actually not so easy for me to operate with them. It's not the law yet, plus my glasses fog up. I get overheated. I don't breathe that well when I wear one. I know, I sound like an old Jewish grandmother. So except for work and the grocery store, I haven't worn a mask the rest of the time. Now when I say the rest of the time, let's not get carried away and get all angry at me. All I get to do is hike, walk, grab coffee, and go to my mailbox down the street. But in those scant moments, people stare me down as if I was taking a shit on their front lawn.

But I got the stinky eye long for other things long before Corona, so I guess I'm used to it. The worst was when I used to be an Orthdoox Jew.

Beep, beep . . . Beep, beep . . . Beep, beep . . .

"Sir, please step over here to my right. You've been randomly selected for additional security screening."

The first time I'd been asked to go through a random screening at St. Louis Lambert International Airport after the metal detector went off, I wasn't at all mad. It was about a year after 9/11 and I thought if this is what they need to do to keep us safe, I'm willing to play along. I was headed to a court hearing in Miami and was more focused on my work trip anyway.

"Are you okay with us doing the screening here, or would you prefer a private room?" the male private screener politely but stoically asked me before touching me. The screener was no taller than five-foot four, chubby, and wore thick, almost coke-bottle type glasses. Buzz-cut, military-style, straight dirty blond hair. Didn't crack a smile, although I doubt that would've made things better. His employee tag read "W. Mueller." It was two in the afternoon and he was visibly sweating from the overheated airport security area. The last thing I wanted was a private room with a short sweating German guy named

Mueller. Jeffrey the Jew and Mueller the German Groper. No thanks.

"I'm okay doing it right here," I responded in a *let's get this fucking over with* tone.

"Okay. I'm going to be touching you on the insides of your thighs and on your buttocks," Mueller warned before he began.

Mueller's blue latex-glove covered hands slid up and down my inner thighs, grazing my scrotum, down my legs, back up my calves, and up the sides of my ass. Then he slid them just inside the waist of my jeans, around the circumference of my body. I didn't know whether to be thankful some people were willing to feel up other men for their career as a sacrifice to our country, or to be grossed out by the whole thing. It dawned on me then that strippers also feel up others for their career, but obviously not for the sake of national security. Would be kind of cool if strippers gave you the TSA-style play by play. "Ready? I'm going to turn around, and then grind my ass into your groin area . . ."

"Okay, all set," Mueller said, satisfied after he was finished violating my dignity. "You can grab your backpack."

I still was sorta glad our country was taking steps to protect us, but the Mueller rubdown wasn't exactly a fun start to my day. I wanted a shower but that still isn't a post-screening option at any airport I've ever been to. Maybe they have that in Dubai or something. I hear that have that option in first class on their airplanes.

I've never been into pigeonhole labels since not everyone in every group is the same, but my status as a religious Jew essentially in 2002 meant that except for work, I wore a yarmulke—a Jewish skullcap—everywhere I went. Orthodox Jews believe it's mandatory to wear a covering on our head to remind us that our creator is spiritually *above* us. Yarmulke, while an

English word now, is really a contraction of two Hebrew words, *yari* and *malka*. Yari, meaning fear or awe, and malka, meaning king or queen. In other words, the yarmulke head covering literally means "in awe of the king."

When I was selected for my first random security screening by Herr Mueller, I was wearing a black felt yarmulke on my head, the type and color many ultra-Orthodox Jews typically wear. I wasn't naïve about how some people feel about us Jews, but it never dawned on me anyone was scared we might take down a plane. I have my own complaints about the Orthodox community I decided to leave in 2007. Terrorism just wasn't one of them. Anyway, I didn't connect the random screening with the black thing on my head at that time. I've won contests with worse odds than being chosen by TSA, so I accepted my lot.

Two months later, on my way to Pittsburgh for another work trip, for a lawsuit involving patents on laser guided training rifles for the military, the magical St. Louis airport screening buzzer went off again as I stepped through, metal free. What are the chances, I thought? Randomly selected two trips in a row. Should I start playing the lottery? Maybe the frequency of these types of screenings had increased with the ever-common government orange alerts. Orange meant the threat of a terrorist attack was high and it seemed these were almost daily occurrences then. They probably still are, but I think we've just become numb to the dangers of the world. Or worse, we've learned to accept the new reality.

This time, the designated feeler-upper was Jesus Martinez. Definitely a step up from Mueller. Not that I dreamt of being touched by nice-looking men in airport security lines, or anywhere for that matter, but Jesus was handsome. At least compared to Mueller. He was well groomed. About five-foot nine, with straight black hair. A friendly smile. Muscular arms. And the bonus? Definitely no grandparents who gassed my relatives in Auschwitz. I didn't really know a lot of Hispanic people back then, so his first name stood out. Jesus. I never understood why people from Latin American countries name their kids after their god. I certainly didn't know any white guys growing up in Ohio named Jesus. The closest we ever got was Chris.

The whole Jesus name thing reminds me of this guy Bill in college. Bill lived in a fraternity house next to mine at Ohio State. It was a fraternity for people majoring in agricultural subjects. I didn't really know much about him except I knew he was from Marietta, Ohio and we would sometimes exchange a passing hello here or there when we saw each other leaving for class. He was majoring in animal husbandry, which actually sounded disgusting in a bestiality kind of way, but I learned it was just a farm animal breeding program. He wasn't going to marry a horse.

It wasn't until the spring quarter of our junior year that Bill and I actually had a class together, which wasn't weird since Ohio State had fifty thousand undergrads. We were taking Women's Studies 201. I only remember because Bill couldn't stand the class. All this talk about equal pay, homosexuality, female empowerment and the like got under his skin. He incessantly fought our teacher Janet on just about every subject. "Marriage is between a man and a woman," he once admonished our lesbian professor in front of the entire class. I had the *pleasure* of listening to his kvetching about these topics on our walk back from class two times a week. Occasionally, he would throw in an extra jab at other minorities. A joke here or there about Black folks. Asian jokes. Even a Jewish joke once, although he quickly remembered his audience—me—and punched my arm. "You know I'm just kidding, Jeff, right?" Yes. Hilarious.

After our last class of the quarter, I decided to challenge my small-minded friend.

"Can I ask you a question, Bill?"

"Sure, what's up," he responded, visibly happy he was finally done with the class.

"I want to get something straight. You worship a dark-skinned Jewish guy, but you don't care much for dark-skinned people or Jews, do you? How do you reconcile that?"

Bill had a confused look on his face. "What the fuck are you talking about?"

"Well, I assume you know that Jesus wasn't from Norway or Sweden or Germany. He was from the Middle East. And I assume that, unlike Michelangelo, you know what people from the Middle East look like. On top of that, Jesus was Jewish. Let me lay it out there nice and easy for you. Jesus was a dark-skinned Jew."

Bill just looked at me with piercing eyes, said a quick "you're an asshole," and walked away. I moved that summer and never ran into him again the following year.

Jesus Martinez's airport pat-down wasn't only a step up from Mueller's because he was easier on the eyes. He also managed to spare "accidentally" grazing my balls. Plus, Martinez understood how unpleasant it was. "Hey man, sorry about this. Just have to be safe. Have a good day." The entire experience was much less invasive than Mueller's that I forgot I had just been chosen for random screenings two trips in a row. That was until my very next work trip three weeks later.

I made it through St. Louis's airport screening on a trip to Little Rock without incident, but my return the next evening didn't go quite as smoothly. Maybe it was foolish of me to wear my yarmulke in Arkansas, but I calmly stepped through the metal detector at Adams Field. You guessed it. Randomly selected again.

Adams Field was originally named after a famous captain in the Arkansas National Guard who was killed in the line of duty in the 1930s. It was later named Clinton Airport after Bill and Hillary in 2012. Had it already been named Clinton Airport when I visited, I guess I could've expected to be felt up in honor of Bill, but back in 2003 I had no such worry. This time a female TSA agent stopped me. "Excuse me, sir," she loudly said in a thick Southern accent. "Y'all gonna need to step over here," as she shooed me to the left of her. Then she took out her walkie-talkie. "We have a male random in line two." There was that word again. Random. For some reason, I didn't feel like I had won anything despite being searched three trips in a row. Plus, couldn't she just do it? Why did I have to wait for a man? Couldn't they just ask my sexual preference first?

This time the name badge on my would-be groper was, no joke, "Lt. R. Lee." I mean are you fucking kidding me. First I get groped by SS guard Mueller and now, while in the deep south, Robert E. Lee? Maybe his first name was Ralph or Riley or even Roger and I was just overreacting. "Okay, son," Lieutenant Lee started. Lee was in his sixties. Tall, maybe six-foot three, thin, a full head of straight gray hair and a thick gray mustache with no other facial hair.

Of the next ten work trips, I got randomly searched on nine of them. Nine random searches on ten trips over two years. I almost wanted to put a mini plastic gun under my yarmulke as a joke. Or maybe have a custom yarmulke made with a picture of a bomb. Or what about wearing an I ♥ Osama sweatshirt? "Aha!!! I knew it! Those dangerous Jews!" I could hear TSA now. Alas, I remember my criminal law professor telling me years ago that there are two groups of people who don't have a sense of humor. Police officers and airport security. Go figure.

I decided to leave the world of Orthodox Judaism when I got divorced in 2007, and something miraculous happened at the same time. Since I stopped walking through airport security lines with a yarmulke, my balls and thighs have been rubbed down a grand total of zero times. (I mean by TSA agents, of course.) Oh, and the other thing that hasn't happened in those same thirteen years? Not one Orthodox Jew has taken down an airplane. Wild.

Rona Day 41, Entry 2

I'm convinced I already had Corona after my trip to northern California mid-January to go to Napa with my girlfriend. Within two weeks of my return, I was sicker than I had been in a decade. Recovered just fine, but boy did that suck. I finally got approved by my physician this week to have an antibodies test to see if I had a fuck you–fighting Corona army in my body already. My doctor says we don't know for sure if that will protect me and others, but typically, that's how viruses work. They attack. We attack back. We win. And then we keep the army we assembled so the virus can't come back.

Rona Day 41, Entry 3

I bet strippers have been hit hardest by Corona.

I saw a sign at one of the clubs I drive by on the way to work that said "We're clothed."

Then on the news the other day, one of the clubs called Shotgun Willie's, which I actually thought was a Western steakhouse when I moved to Denver because of a sign that said T-Bone Tuesdays, held a stripper car wash. I thankfully didn't see it in person, but it was all over social media. It's no shocker that some of those employees don't look as good at two p.m. at Target as they do under the dark black lights. The car wash was no exception.

I don't have anything against strippers. They're people, too. But I never really liked strip clubs that much. You do realize they are pretending and don't reaaaalllly think you're handsome, do you guys?

Rona Day 42

Violent, middle-aged, right-wing, and mostly bearded un-masked white men stormed the Michigan state capitol building today. Some were screaming at police officers inches from their faces, no mask on. One of them took the butt of his gun and whacked a reporter. Oh, what a privilege it must be to walk into a government building armed with loaded guns and not be gunned down while politicians don bulletproof vests. Why of all days is this the day y'all "protestors" chose not to dress up in Black face. Is this what you meant when you said "liberate" Michigan Mr. Trump?

There's been so much talk about rights from these groups lately that maybe I should be feeling optimistic instead of scared. Maybe these will be the same troopers who start standing up for the rights of unarmed Black men before more are gunned down by our government. Maybe they will be the ones who are so passionate about rights that they won't ever vote for a racist politician. Maybe they will be the catalyst for voting rights. Or the tipping point for gay rights. Maybe even women's rights.

I sure hope their newfound passion for rights isn't only about their right to endanger our elderly or at-risk citizens.

I don't want to go out on a limb, but if I could indulge you for just a moment and posit that these folks never laid a finger for civil rights before. Four hundred years of slavery, inequality and inequity. And not a fucking word. But now people are asked to simply stay home a couple months and all hell breaks loose. Boy I'd love to see the Venn diagram for people at the Michigan capitol building and members of bigoted groups like the KKK. The demonstration two weeks prior even featured some lovely swastikas and Confederate flags. Last time I checked, Michigan wasn't even part of the South so I'm guessing it had nothing to do with Southern pride. Did it ever?

Keep calm and stay selfish, dear rights advocates.

Rona Day Whatever: Fuck the Police

Went to Whole Foods at seven this morning and was stopped at the entrance by a cop.

"Excuse me sir, may I see your ID?"

I returned a confused look. "My ID? What do you need my ID for?" I had my mask on. My hands were freshly washed. I hadn't sneezed in over two days. I hadn't left my house except to get coffee. What did I do wrong?

"From six to eight is senior shopping. Age sixty and up."

This was about to be the first time I said Fuck You straight in the face of a police officer.

"What about me made you think I might be 60 or over," I responded in at least a fuck you tone as I walked my 51 year old body towards my car.

I drove by sarcastically waving goodbye to the cop. If corona wasn't enough to ruin an otherwise good day.

I think I'll work out to an Ice-T playlist this morning.

Rona Day Whatever, Entry 2

So confused to see Klan members protesting government Corona rules. They finally got approval to wear their masks and now they're bitching about that, too?

You just can't please people these days.

Rona Day 44: Redemption Day

Pulled up to two stores to buy flowers for the one-year anniversary of my first date with my girlfriend and both times, with no request for my ID, the police officers told me "Sorry, sixty and older shopping until eight." Booya!

You see, blue lives do matter after all.

Happy one year! One of the bright spots of Corona days. Kind of makes you feel bad for all the people who have to endure this mess alone, especially the elderly.

Cherish your loved ones.

Rona Day 45

Been working out at the gym so hard for two years only to find out it's the antibody I really want.

Went to get tested for those bad boys today. I sure hope I had the Rona. Maybe they can give me a special *that cough you had back in January was the Rona* bracelet so I can go wherever I want then.

Rona Day 45, Entry 2

News of unemployment numbers and people having trouble making ends meet due to Corona is upsetting. I recall my own family struggling financially most of my childhood.

Decades before those sex toy parties, my super loving mom was a Tupperware Lady. At least that's what we not-so-polit-ically-correct folk called it back in 1980. Not sure what they call them today. Gender Neutral Tupperware Representatives? Sounds so unappealing. Mom was a teacher, and between her measly $25,000 a year salary and Dad's struggling solo law practice, the family needed extra dough to keep up with the piling credit card bills. So Mom sold Tupperware.

The way it worked wasn't much different than the lube and French tickler gatherings people have today. Mom would find a friend or acquaintance to host a party, that friend would then invite her friends, and then Mom would show off some fabu-lous, new, cutting-edge Tupperware containers. These events were called Tupperware Parties. Not exactly my idea of a party if you ask me, but I guess you serve some Tostitos, spinach dip, and red Kool-Aid after seven and voila, it's a plastic storage bin party. Woo-hoo!!

The cool thing for me as an eleven-year-old was that Mom had all kinds of Tupperware container samples. This was one of the big life perks of being a Tupperware Lady. All sorts of containers with compartments and trays. Tiny ones. Large ones. Flat ones. Tall ones. Any time I needed to organize my preteen life, I just absconded with one of Mom's colorful samples. She never even noticed. I thought I was sly, but really, who would notice missing plastic storage tubs? My favorite one, which I still have nearly forty years later, was a red five by seven inches, two-tiered, and four inches tall container. The top part has a tray with five different shallow compartments, and it includes a tray you can place on top of the rest of the container that covers the lower storage area. I used it for buttons with funny sayings, a few baseball cards, and other small odds and ends.

Not much an eleven-year-old really needs, but I thought it was important at the time. Reagan was just elected president, so I also had one of Dad's Carter-Mondale collector pins. Dad kept telling me and my seven-year-old brother that Reagan was a fascist. I didn't know what that meant, but from Dad's accusatory tone, it sounded like a really bad thing. The only other words I had heard that ended in "ist" were racist, psychologist, and televangelist. None of those had ever appealed to me as potential life paths, so I'm sure fascist fit right in. In my forties, I finally learned that psychologists were pretty good after all, but still gonna pass on racists and Pat Robertson.

Mom eventually gave up on her Tupperware career when everyone she knew and every one of her friends' friends, and probably their friends' friends, had enough plastic containers to last a couple lifetimes. Most of Mom's Jewish friends had more money than us, so it wouldn't surprise me if they bought extra Tupperware they didn't even need, just to help Mom hit her sales quotas. Everyone loved Mom. But we were only one of two Jewish families I knew who didn't live in one of the nicer neighborhoods. It sucked trying to keep up with the Goldsteins all those years. It's not that our affluent Jewish friends were bad people, but the contrast between their large homes, Florida vacations, and fancy cars and our tiny chateau, four-cylinder Datsun 210 stick shift and Ohio state park adventures was stark.

When the three hundred dollars a month Tupperware gravy train dried up, Mom turned to Avon. Yeah, you guessed it, she officially transitioned into the Avon Lady. Avon has a line of creams, makeup, and other beauty products, mostly for women. Avon wasn't that interesting to me since I didn't have much use for Mom's boxes of lipstick and eyeliner samples. I once looked through a catalog and sprayed my preteen face with some musk, vomit-inducing, Old Spice–smelling cologne after overhearing Mom talk to someone on the phone about a new men's line.

I couldn't even look through Mom's sample box without gagging. The intermingling of open bottles of Avon's Imari, Sweet Honesty, Timeless, and Ariane perfumes was more than enough to postpone any serious interest in girls for at least another year. Okay, maybe not, but I knew I wouldn't match up well with the types of girls who showered in that muck. After college I went on a date with a girl who must've sprayed herself with an entire bottle of old lady perfume, something called *Charlie*, and I couldn't stop coughing the entire evening.

One of the side benefits from Mom's Avon stint was that I was twelve and got to babysit my younger brother Aaron while Mom promoted beauty products at Avon parties a few times a week. Dad usually had to work late as well, so we had the house all to ourselves. I was in charge of cooking dinner, making sure we did whatever occasional homework Yorktown Middle School and Olde Orchard Elementary assigned us, and then picking the TV shows my brother and I would watch until bedtime. *The Jeffersons*, *Three's Company*, *The Greatest American Hero*, an occasional episode of the Confederate flag–boasting *The Dukes of Hazzard*, *Chips*, *Different Strokes*, reruns of *Sanford and Son*, *Gimme a Break!* and several others.

My brother and I already were addicted to television, but now we really had no limits. All while also getting to eat

Swanson TV dinners. Fried chicken, mash potatoes, some corn carrot medley, and of course a brownie for dessert. I was really loving this Avon gig despite the boring product line.

I imagine the Avon job ended when Mom's Tupperware customers finally filled their Tupperware bins with too many useless beauty products. We wondered how Mom was going to earn extra money when the number of our Avon-sponsored free nights at home dwindled to once a month. I knew our family was still struggling when arguments over money began increasing threefold after she stopped selling Avon.

That's when Mom turned to Sarah Coventry Jewelry. It no longer exists today, but back then Sarah Coventry was a line of cheap costume jewelry. Mom showed up one day with boxes of necklaces, bracelets, earrings, Christmas jewelry, rings, and every other imaginable adornment. As usual, I secretly scoured through the boxes to see if anything was ripe for the taking.

No luck except a ring with a giant sparkly gold dollar sign on top. I was in eighth grade and had just developed a crush on this girl Denise. Thin. Short blonde hair. A friendly smile. I was knee deep in my ugly stage with a blow dried and nappy Jewish mop on my head. And I was short, too, to make matters worse. Even though Denise was known as one of the cuter girls at Yorktown, she at least acknowledged my presence, much to my disbelief. Midway through the year I finally got up my nerve. I wrote her a note asking her to go with me and handed her the drab dollar sign ring.

My preteen brain and emotions thought it was a really romantic gift back then. Denise thought so, too, or at least she was good at feigning interest. "It's beautiful, Jeff! I love it." She gave me a long, deep hug but still didn't answer my initial question. All I ended up getting out of the deal was the hug and a nice note with a phone number to call her over the summer. I lost the note of course, and that was the last year Denise attended school with me. I never saw her again. As luck would have it, I never even knew her last name.

Denise wasn't the only teenage trauma Sarah Coventry played a part in. Hoop earring customer Mrs. Williamson was far worse. Mom sometimes took me and my brother with her to deliver the jewelry to all the middle-aged white women who purchased something at one of the various host parties. It was such a pain in the ass driving all over creation with Mom, watching her drop off the junky jewelry. "Do we have to go this time?" I complained one typical summer day. "Oh, just come with me," Mom begged.

We loved spending time with Mom, but not this way. "Mrs. Williamson only lives a few blocks away." That was a lot better than the thirty-minute drives across town, so I acquiesced. I had no idea what I was getting into. We pulled up to a mobile home park. Banged up cars. Old model pickup trucks. A loud barking pit bull chained to a metal fence. Trash everywhere. I didn't even realize there were mobile homes a mere hundred yards from our home, hidden two streets over off Main Street.

We pulled up to Mrs. Williamson's double-wide, dark gray painted home. The door was open, but Mom lightly knocked anyway before walking in. "Well come on in, Irene," a voice delightfully called out as if she was thrilled to have any visitor. I followed closely behind Mom, since as financially strapped as our family was, we still didn't have our house delivered on wheels. I peeked around Mom, horrified at the sight of the place. There was shit everywhere. Like the place had never been cleaned, and the smell was so pungently awful it took every ounce of energy just to keep myself from vomiting on Mrs. Williamson's already stained dark red carpet.

Apparently I wasn't the first one to unload breakfast on the floor there. I couldn't tell if the smell was from the unkempt hamster cage, the dirty dishes piled three feet high and overflowing from the sink, or her unwashed oversized clothes tossed around the place. Mrs. Williamson lived alone and didn't get up when she welcomed us into her abode. She was a good four hundred pounds and sat sunken deep into one of those large La-Z-Boy chairs with a footrest that moves up and down. Mrs. Williamson had her feet propped up, and you could see purple veins running down her exposed calves. The chair was a faded pink but had brown stains down the side. Another possible source for the nauseating smell, I thought to myself.

Up until this point, I was sorta mad and even embarrassed our proudly Jewish family didn't have any money like most of the other Jews we knew. But after seeing Mrs. Williamson's home, I couldn't wait to get back to our 1,400 square-foot and stationary one-car garage home. Our house wasn't the cleanest one on the block, but it was Buckingham Palace compared to the smelly double-wide. I never felt bad about our house, our shitty car, or our cracked pavement street ever again. Well, at least for a while, but I still can't get the Williamson smell out of my mind almost four decades later. It remained a reminder throughout the rest of my childhood that no matter how little we had, there were people out there who struggled far, far worse. Especially these days.

By the time I started high school, Mom retired from her career as a jewelry pusher and every other party-sold ware. No more dollar sign rings. No more plastic containers. No more sparkly eye shadow. And thankfully, no more nauseating smells.

The struggle was real, though.

Rona Day 46

"You spin me right round, baby
    Right round like a record, baby
    Right round round round"

I was never a fan of cheesy '80s music, except of course rap and R&B. I mean, really people? REO Speedwagon? Air Supply? Journey? C'mon. You can't really enjoy that music, can you? I think you cling to it like a childhood memory more than because the music is actually good. But these days I can't get the group Dead or Alive's one-hit wonder out of my head. The world is spinning so fast I can't even fathom what's coming our way next.

Rona Day 47

Not gonna lie. I can't stand wearing the masks we're required to don in any business. You definitely don't hear things like "you have a nice smile" anymore.

Rona Day 49

Guess those eyes-only showing burkas aren't so offensive to Americans after all.

Rona Day 50

It's a miracle.
    Corona has finally done what nobody else could do. So many have tried, but only an invisible virus that had to travel from the dog, bat, and pangolin wet markets of China were

able to unify the extreme anarchist left and angry right in America. Whatever separates them on other issues, such as race, race, or race, Corona conquered.

That's right. Left and right-wingers have united to promote no less than seven (my count) conspiracy theories as to why the virus, or hoax in some cases, is here.

Of course, my favorite is always The Jews Did It theory. But not far behind is one shared by one of my Jewish right-wing friends—that the elite have gotten together to bring Corona to us. Forget that most of these elite just lost their asses in the stock market and some of their companies are now on the verge of bankruptcy. I asked my *elite theory* Jewish friend who these elite people were that were meeting at remote locations to come and get us. I asked if any of their names ended in Stein, or Soros, or maybe Rothschild. Silence on the other end of our phone call.

"Jon, you do realize that The Jews Did It crowd and the The Elite Did It crowd are basically the same. Be careful which direction you walk," I warned him.

A far-left almost anarchist acquaintance on social media, also Jewish, had similarly just posted about how a group of about ten Jews were in control of everything and caused this mess.

My response to Trisha wasn't as respectful: "That's absurd. I can't believe you peddle in that blatant anti-Semitism."

Her only response was, "I've been called an anti-Semite before." But then again, there were a tiny group of asshole Jews who helped the Nazis in WWII, too, so what's a freedom fighter to do?

Reminds me of one of my favorite jokes.

Two elderly Jews, Sol and Bernie, were sitting on a park bench in New York where they typically kibbitz for an hour each day. "Kibbitz" for you non-Jewish folk means chitchat.

Sol looked over at Bernie. "Bernie, what the hell are you reading? You normally have *The New York Times* or *The Washington Post*. Why are you reading that Shmata."

Bernie was reading the Nation of Islam's *The Final Call* newspaper. A notoriously anti-Semitic rag (shmata in Yiddish) that blames the Jews on everything from Kennedy's assassination to the World Trade Center bombing to the African slave trade. Total madness.

Sol responded to Bernie without a blink. "When I read *The New York Times*, I see swastikas being painted on Jewish gravestones in Europe, Israel is engaged in another war, a synagogue was shot up in Australia. The UN voting against Israel again. Always something bad happening to the Jews. Things are awful. When I read Farrakhan's *The Final Call*, we own the banks, we control the media, we run the world, we own all the money. It's vonderful. Vonderful I tell you, Bernie!"

Sadly, the Jews are blamed for so many things, it gets exhausting. All I know is I was certainly never given my Jewish ATM pin number to Bank of the Jews.

The conspiracy theories about Corona don't get any better from there.

My second favorite is the documentary about a scientist who was essentially kicked out of every science institution in the world. She claims in this "movie" that pharmaceutical companies started the virus so they could force us all to take their eventual Corona vaccine and make a gazillion dollars off us. The thing that makes this claim so credible is the super spooky music that plays in the background of the movie.

If you're gonna post any conspiracy theory videos online, definitely only do so if they include really scary music in the background. It helps make more plausible the theory you're promoting. Shit, I was even scared at one point. Anyway, according to this theory, pharma was going to get rich this way. Wait. Big Pharma is already rich, and 98% of their profits come from us staying sick, not from curing shit. Duh. So even if you were going to create some large pharma connect-the-dots movie, you could at least accuse them of keeping us sick on drugs instead. Plus, I'm pretty sure two months of stay-at-home orders is enough to scare us into the vaccine, so where is it already? I actually thought the Big Pharma documentary was a comedy there were so many holes in it, but alas people believe that crap more often than bat cacciatore is served in Wuhan.

Of course, the conspiracy folks aren't virologists. Not epidemiologists. Not our world or nation's health organizations. Not our top doctors. Just your average right- and left-wing extremists. But, duh, that's because the WHO, the CDC, the top virus-fighting agencies in the world, the top epidemiologists, and the doctors are all in on it. What the fuck do you think happens at medical conferences? Every last one of them is plotting against us? C'mon people.

Now back to our regularly scheduled programming. Can we please get back to thinking for ourselves, and enough with the spooky background music?

The rest of the other Corona conspiracy theories hold up even less. I won't get into all of them, but my second favorite after *blame the Jews* is that this is a conspiracy to bring down Donald Trump. First it was the couple dozen administration and campaign officials indicted for a whole host of crimes. Then it was paying off porn stars. Refusing to fund Ukraine unless they take down the Bidens.

None of that fake news worked, so now let's get serious and just create a virus. Yes, that bearded guy in Boulder still playing hacky sack, along with his surfer friend in Santa Cruz high on weed, are virus creators on weekends. I'm sure they had to work really hard and fast on making the virus since most of us thought Trump would never survive the previous record number of scandals. Who knew we'd actually need a virus to topple him? What's funny is the take-Trump-out theorists don't all agree. Some think COVID-19 is made up. Others think Corona has been exaggerated on purpose to tank the economy so 45 loses.

Others think the virus is real, but it was made in a lab on purpose to screw Trump out of reelection. I actually saw a Facebook post that said this was the nineteenth version of the virus before they got it right. I can't keep up with the twists and turns on this but either way, the virus's number one enemy is Donald Trump according to these camps. Probably was a coincidence that COVID-19 was discovered in, wait for it… 2019.

The list of conspiracy theories abounds, but the quirky thing about it is that I'm watching Trump supporters and the leftist Bernie gang post the same bizarre theories. So I guess we owe some thanks to Corona. You were able to unify two of the most polar opposite groups in the country. Maybe they'll make a deal. The left will temporarily set aside calling all Trump supporters racists and the right will stop calling the Bernie bunch radical socialists. Then they can focus on the real issue. Which conspiracy is the truth? So many to choose from.

Rona Mother Day's 2020

Seeing lots of OCD these days. Obsessive-Corona disorder.

Where you constantly obsess with proving Corona is a conspiracy, an exaggeration, a hoax, or simply no big deal.

Hey, what are you looking at? Okay, I know. I write about Corona every day. So maybe I need help, too. After you

OCDers get the therapy you sorely need, how about you send some recommendations my way.

Rona Day 55

I haven't written in a few days. I guess when I got my antibodies test results back last week, I wasn't feeling all that funny.

I logged on to National Jewish Health's system to get my results with excited anticipation. I was thoroughly convinced I already had the virus. Then I clicked on the "Results" button:

BORDERLINE.

Borderline? What kind of result is that? You may or may not have had Corona? You may or may not be immune? You may or may not have wasted your time going through the drive-thru blood lab? What the fuck is borderline?

I called a few doctor friends, and their opinions ranged from "You probably had a different coronavirus at some point in your life but you didn't meet the threshold to say that you had this one" to "You likely had COVID-19 but your body is still developing the rest of the antibodies so we will test again in a few weeks."

So I'm borderline on having the antibodies. And today after doing a hundred sit-ups, a hundred deadlifts, a hundred squats, and a hundred rows, I borderline almost threw up. And just a few minutes ago at my coffee shop I asked for my coffee "to go," as if I had another option right now. Borderline dumbass now, too! Starting to see a pattern.

Rona Day 56

I'm thinking about throwing a giant Facebook block party soon. Nah, not one of those online happy hours on Zoom where you can watch people get drunk in a one-inch square box, but the kind where I just go through my list of so-called online friends and start blocking people.

Corona has seriously driven people batshit crazy. Pun intended. Yesterday a person I went to high school with was posting about some tiny group of Jews controlling the world and being responsible for all the bad shit going down. When I confronted her absurd anti-Semitism, all she could say was "I wasn't referring to all Jews," to which I responded, "Then why even mention the religion of someone you don't like unless the religion is causing the supposed problem?" Her response, "Well, they all are Jewish." Oy vey. Hey, hey, surprise surprise. She wasn't our valedictorian.

Rona Day 57: Don't Be A Maskhole

I remember the day well. The afternoon of June 26, 2009. It was a sweltering 99 degrees in St. Louis. I had just happened upon a discussion at Starbucks between an acquaintance, Matt, and a group of men I had never seen. Don't worry, my taste in coffee has improved since then.

Matt was the most self-described conservative I had ever met. He was belligerently lecturing this group on why climate change wasn't real. I couldn't help myself, so I chimed in with a sarcastic smile.

"Matt, I thought you were a conservative. You know, not one of those loosey goosey high risk liberals. Conservative. Cautious. Careful."

"I am," he proudly and firmly responded, not realizing the bait I had just set for him.

"You'd agree neither of us are climate scientists. Neither of us have ever obtained any degrees in environmental studies or climate science, right?"

I didn't wait for his answer to my rhetorical question. I already knew Matt was a bankruptcy lawyer and didn't have the letters Ph and D after his last name.

"And you'd agree that the best either of us can do is rely on what experts say on the topic, right?"

He nodded his head, as I continue to lead him down the path.

"But if most of the world climate scientists are wrong," I continued, "and climate change either isn't real or its just cyclical and not related to human actions, as you say, then the worst thing we did by implementing environmental safeguards is made cleaner air, cleaner water and a cleaner planet. Maybe even wasted some money."

"If you're wrong, though, and we do nothing regarding our planet, and it turns out the thousands of climate PhDs are right, we could cause irreparable damage to our planet. Wouldn't you want to be conservative and play it safe. Not be so liberal and callous with our planet. Gosh, what if the naysayers like you and Fox News are wrong and we just let the planet slide into something irreversible."

"You see, Matt, that's why the word conservation and conservative come from the same origin. I for one think we should pay it safe and be conservative with our planet."

Now we have COVID-19 and it's largely the same people who reject human induced climate change that think the whole mask wearing thing is absurd. Mostly self-described conservatives again.

I'm no virologist or epidemiologist. I wouldn't be able to peer review any studies from doctors.

But I'm conservative when it comes to the health and well-being of my fellow humans. I don't believe in acting loosey goosey liberal when it comes to the most vulnerable people in society.

So when the World Health Organization, the Center for Disease Control and most of the top virologists and epidemiologists worldwide say we can speed through the virus and help protect people if we all wear masks, I really have no independent basis to accept or reject their studied opinions.

What I do know is that if these experts are wrong, but we take their advice anyway and wear masks, we will have looked silly and been made uncomfortable and inconvenienced for a while.

If it turns out by some odd change they are right, but we decided instead to ignore their advice, we will end up overwhelming our hospital systems and unnecessarily killing our fellow Americans. Including people we love.

So let's be conservative when it comes to wearing masks. Let' not play liberal roulette with others' lives.

If not for yourself, do it for your fellow human beings. It's not like it's September 16, 1940 and you're being required to fight the Germans in a world war across the Atlantic.

It's a fucking mask.

Rona Day 58

Masks have been mandatory in businesses for a while now. I still despise them, but I guess they are better than a one thousand dollar fine per droplet. Mine are either black or white. Nothing stylistic, although occasionally I wear a bandana. I ordered Ohio State masks over a month ago, but they haven't arrived. Probably a scam, but who has time to check these days? Oh wait. We all do. Now you know it wasn't your supposed busy schedule why those house projects got pushed off the last two years.

My only daily interaction outside the house is my three-minute stop to get coffee where I typically run into the regulars there.

"How have you been doing," seems to be the only conversation left in everyone's arsenal, albeit muffled through the cloth mask. And "I'm so sick of this shit," is the only response left. Well, that and "I'm sorry, what did you say?" Half the time you can't even understand people nowadays.

"Oh, I miss going to parties," I once said to barista Rachel.

"You want two vanilla lattes?" she asked back. What the fuck.

Those damn masks. And just wait until it's 102 degrees outside, then see how fun they are. Still haven't figured out why so many people wear them alone in their cars. That line between public safety and sheeplehood.

Still, the brief moment to venture out into Zombieland for coffee is my favorite part of the day now. I get extra excited when the line is three people deep. That means I get an extra three to four minutes of human time. Sometimes I even feign mulling over what I will order to extend my stay. "What should I get today…let me think," as Patrick, Alex, James, or Hayden annoyingly wait for me to tell them my order. As if I might mix it up today, which never happens. I still prefer my straight foo-foo $4.32 twelve-ounce coffee. Rwandan today.

Rona Day 57

Even though I probably would've flunked out of med school since I can't stand the sight of blood and, to be honest, I couldn't stand the sight of books either in my college years, I've been sorta wishing I had become a virologist.

There is just so much information bombarding us every day that I can't always make heads or tails of everything. To most though, the words "I don't know" are a thing of the past. It's depressing to see how many car salesmen, mechanics, painters, lawyers, office managers and the like are now experts on how viruses work. How they all know what the true death numbers are. Not the World Health Organization or our own CDC, but *The Washington Times* or *Drudge Report* have the real numbers. They all seem to know what our hospitals can handle. They all know how best to reopen society. The breadth of their expertise is impressive. I'm starting to be proud to include them in my list of friends even.

I'm not going to lie. I've fallen prey to the misinformation disease myself. My friend Clayton posted a video that had a headline on the link about Corona all being a hoax and I just commented back "Not you, too!" He asked if I had watched the video. In my defense, I had seen so many of the bullshit conspiracy videos, I just thought this was a repeat and said "Yes!" Someone else asked if I had clicked on the link. I hadn't, but now something seemed fishy. I clicked the weirdo conspiracy video and it was nothing more than a music video.

"Never gonna give you up
Never gonna let you down
Never gonna run around and desert you
Never gonna make you cry
Never gonna say goodbye
Never gonna tell a lie and hurt you"

Yeah, you guessed it. It was just one-hit wonder Rick Astley's sole hit song from the '80s. I was punked! Here I had spent four back-and-forths debating people over conspiracy theories and finally, it was just a good ole fashioned prank.

I typically don't fall for that kind of crap, but it seems we all have become advocates on one side of the Corona battle or another. Will the real sheep please stand up? Never mind. Sheep can't stand up on two legs. I guess that's why they're called sheep.

Rona Day 58

I can't keep the days straight anymore. Today is technically Thursday, but I only know that because I thought yesterday was Thursday and today is Friday. Either way, I found my new job. I'm a personal assistant to my three teenagers.

"Good morning everyone!"

Teenage son number one: "Good morning [pauses]. Can you go to the store and get me some more milk? I like to drink four to five glasses a day. Oh, and what's for lunch today? I have a twelve-thirty Zoom class, so if we could eat around noon that would be best. Also, can you text Grandma and Grandpa and let them know we can FaceTime at seven?"

Teenage daughter: "I saved a dress I want online, so maybe you could take a look and have it shipped here, if it's not too expensive. Also, can you run me over to Mommy's after four? I have an appointment on Google Hangouts. And could you print out the essay I wrote for English class and help me proofread?"

And teenage son number two texts me, "Have you already left for coffee? Would you mind picking me up on your way home? Thanks. ☺"

The smiley face at the end is like getting a star sticker from your teacher. Okay, I feel good now.

It's not that my kids are difficult. I actually lucked out. They are kind, compassionate, and respectful. Okay, my fifteen-year-old teenage daughter is a bit sassy these days, but other than that, I'm blessed. I'm enjoying all the Rona-induced time I get with them now, but my role definitely feels like I'm no longer the boss anymore.

Rona Day 58, Entry 2: "You Ain't Black"

Well, good ole Joe Biden just proclaimed today that people of color who don't vote for him, in his words, "ain't Black."

Bill Clinton and Donald Trump both love to stuff their faces with high-carb, high-cholesterol, sugar-laced food. Bill's faves were jalapeño cheeseburgers, French fries, chicken enchiladas, and cinnamon rolls. Trump prefers Big Macs (usually two in one meal), Filet-O-Fish, chocolate shakes, KFC, pizza, and, well, Diet Coke, as if the diet part matters at that point. I hear he drinks twelve of those a day. Reagan stuffed his face with Jelly Belly jelly beans and mac 'n' cheese. The late George Bush made it clear broccoli would never end up on his plate. Thomas Jefferson was a huge fan of waffles. Honest Abe devoured gingerbread. FDR munched down on bread pudding and doughnuts. And LBJ couldn't stay away from country-fried steak.

But what would a Biden White House serve up? You see, Joe prefers a different kind of fare. He eats feet.

According to Joe just this past August, "Poor kids are just as bright as white kids."

It wasn't Joe's first racial gaff, and while he's been known to trip over his words for decades, c'mon Joe, really? Tell us how you really feel about people of color. He must've missed the part about the thirty-five million Black people *not* in poverty in this country, or the 15.7 million whites in poverty. Or his former boss. Black doesn't equal poor and that shit doesn't just slip out of your mouth if it isn't in your psyche somewhere. It's not like he accidentally said *well* instead of *good*. Or that he typed *your* instead of *you're*. My gut tells me he didn't mean exactly what was barfed up, but he still wasn't administering the right kind of meds for the never-ending racism pandemic.

Now, had Joe not said in the 1970s that he'd "be damned if I feel responsible to pay for what happened three hundred years ago," I might believe he just has trouble with the English language and sometimes says the wrong thing. To figure out how *woke* Joe might now deal with addressing the legacy of slavery, he was asked about his 1970s comment in 2019, a month after his "all Blacks are poor" implication, he gaffed again. Doubled down to give a paternal lecture on how Black dads and moms could be better parents. Seemed like he still wanted to shirk responsibility. Or did he just say things unartfully again?

This past week, when Joe decided to let us know on Charlamagne Tha God's popular radio talk show *The Breakfast Clu* that anyone who isn't supporting him for president "ain't Black," he put the exclamation point on a long career of offensive racial comments. From criminals in hoodies and gangbanger comments. To justifying cooperation with segregationist senators. Even in 2007 he said Obama was "the first mainstream African American who is articulate and bright and clean." What? How does that type of nonsense, and frankly an outright lie, just slip out?

Don't get me wrong. It's laughable how Trump and his *Fox and Friends* cronies feign concern over Biden's attitude toward Black people. Shithole countries. Least racist person you've ever encountered. Good people on both sides. Stephen Miller. Bannon. Mexican rapists. Judges of Mexican heritage. The birther movement. Trump Management Company's policy of not renting to African Americans. The Central Park Five. Randal Pinkett. "Go back to their huts." I want short Jewish guys in yarmulkes counting my money. A complete shutdown of Muslim immigration. Refusing to criticize David Duke.

We've got a man in the White House who literally gives renewed voice to white supremacists and a presidential stamp of approval for everyday racism. This isn't about whether Trump's a bigot. We'll save that for Trump's next offensive.

I'm sure we can once again explain away Joe's latest "ain't Black" comment. That it was only meant to convey what most Black folks believe anyway. That how on earth could someone of color support a man who's made a mockery of racial progress. It's a fair point. Truth be told, most of us antiracists might rather have Joe at 35% capacity than 45 running on all his unending offensive Big Mac–fueled cylinders.

But should our standard dip to "Is someone less racist or offensive than Trump?" If we've been reduced to that, there's little hope of really addressing the systems of racial inequity that still plague our struggling nation.

When they aim low, we still need to aim high. How about next time, way, way, higher.

Rona Day 59

I've experienced my share of anti-Semitism over the years, but these masks have reminded me of something important. When I walk into a bank, or go to the store, or apply for a mortgage loan, or drive too fast in my car, I don't have a label on my forehead that says *Jew*. While I wear my Jewishness proudly, the average stranger, cop, or loan officer has no idea unless I volunteer the information. Nowadays we're all wearing masks. I can't really get used to them myself. But I can take my Jew mask off anytime I want. The same way the Italians and Irish could remove theirs.

Imagine being Black. Permanent mask. Nowhere to run. May even impede breathing from time to time. My family surname was Koussevitsky when we immigrated to the U.S. in the early 1900s. Changed to Kass, thank God. Would've really fucked up my dating life. Pretty sure if my friend Ryan changed his last name to O'Reilly, though, he'd still pass for Black.

Rona Day 60

Nail salons have reopened. Fuck. I just bought stock in the company that owns Lee press-on nails, too.

Rona Day 61

I have a confession to make. My neighbor is a hair stylist. Brett, we'll call him, so he doesn't get arrested. With my nappy-ass dry curly fro-brillo-pad hair, there was no way in hell I was going three months without a haircut. I'd rather get the Rona than have to look in the mirror like that. He dips my head in his kitchen sink, washes and conditions, then we move to his dining room where he brings me back from a two to a six on the one to ten rating scale. Sometimes I hit a seven if I'm lucky—a number I've been lucky enough to reach maybe four times in fifty-one years.

Rona Day 62

I finally found a good place to write again. Since I can't write in to-go only coffee shops, which is normally where I get the best writing done, today I grabbed my coffee, found a bench outside down the street, and wrote away. Finally, my favorite pastime is back. People watching. As I sat on the bench and watched ridiculously rich white folks in their Lululemon yoga pants walk by with their pure bred perfectly shaved Labra-doodles dressed in Gucci doggie clothes, I felt creative again. I never thought these words would ever leave my lips, but thank you, white people. Thank you thank you, white people. You've restored me.

I wish the Gucci dog clothing comment was a joke, but last week a burly looking dude in a way too tight Dolce & Gabbana sweat suit showed up to get coffee with his four pound dog, fit only for a purse at Neiman Marcus. The white Maltese was full clad in a Gucci outfit with Dolce & Gabbana sunglasses to match his owner. Boy I wish I was kidding right now.

Meanwhile, in downtown Denver, there's a homeless person in need of a regular Merona-branded shirt from Target and some George shoes from Walmart.

Rona Day 63

"All I want to do is zoom-a-zoom-zoom-zoom . . ."

Wreckx-n-Effect was a pure genius psychic. Rump shaker. 1992. And now in 2020 all we ever want to do is zoom-a-zoom. It's the only way I get to see the faces of friends these days. Well, that and airbrushed, Instagram filtered versions, if that counts even. The only thing more brilliant would've been if the song went *All I want to do is Google Hangout.*

I wish Zoom would add an Oscars wrap-up soundtrack that starts playing if you talk too much.

Off to my next virtual meeting.

Rona Day 64

The alleged spotting of alien aircraft released by our government last month got me thinking. Why the fuck would any alien want to stop by our mess of a planet? Wars. Racism. Terrorism. Disease. Pollution. Nazis. People eating pangolins. No way in hell some alien wants our shit. Nice try, but I'm not buying it.

And anyway, why is that every picture we've ever seen of the Loch Ness Monster, Big Foot, Sasquatch and, yes, UFOs, are all blurry as fuck. Seriously. We have satellite capability to take crystal clear pictures of a sign on a front lawn from outer space. Google Maps shows us pictures of cars parked where you can almost read license plates from miles away. We have cameras that can immerse a thousand feet under water and capture some of the most wildest beauty of our wonderous world. Amazing, clear videos of lions chasing gazelles. But nope. When it comes to UFOs and Loch Ness, we only get blurry shots. Those sneaky aliens.

Rona Day 65

I learned a new word today. Covidiots.

My friend Brad, who is an entrepreneur and helps people find the perfect car at the perfect price, has been incessantly and obsessively urging people online not to wear masks.

I replied to his latest post, "Let's see. Should I go with three close doctor friends and a college buddy who is a world-renown epidemiologist or Brad the car broker. Tough call."

Rona Day 66: Barack and Kobe

So many famous people weighing in on COVID and racism these days. Brought me back to some lucky and unlucky interactions with a few celebrities.

A group of friends and I would often hang out at the lounge inside the Ritz Carlton in Clayton, a posh suburb of St. Louis. Overpriced drinks. Subpar food. And way too many white people in one place, especially in St. Louis. But the couches at the Ritz were super comfortable. So much so I once fell asleep on one when the conversations got boring. The live music was usually pretty decent, and it was sort of the place to see and be seen each weekend. At least back in November 1998. Plus, two six-foot something men dressed in high heels as women would usually dance the night away, and in the '90s, that was entertainment enough for our group.

"Holy shit Jeffrey," my friend Lainie said to me as she pointed to a set of couches in the corner of the lounge, directly next to the five-foot-tall fancy fireplace. None other than the new homerun record breaker, St. Louis Cardinal Mark McGwire, was sitting with a few friends. I glanced over. He was easy to spot with his overly muscular frame, gigantic thigh-sized arms, small squinty blue eyes, and his signature reddish goatee. This was before McGwire got busted for cheating in baseball by using performance-enhancing drugs. In other words, he was still a rock star to St. Louisans, having just shattered the single season homerun record by swatting seventy of them. "Oh my gosh. I wish I could meet him," Lainie continued like a little kid who just saw Mickey Mouse at Disneyland.

Anyone who knows me even from my teenage years knows that I don't have too many fears in life. Okay, I'm scared stiff of heights and won't go on a chair lift or roller coaster, or jump out of any planes. But beyond that, I'm more fearless than most. I certainly wasn't afraid of going up to anyone to say hello, play a joke, fake an accent or whatever. My friend Jason in high school always told me one day I'd get my ass kicked for my unfiltered mouth. Now at age fifty-one, I still have escaped the beating he promised. Hoping he remains wrong as I'm not one for pain.

"I'll be right back," I told Lainie as I promptly stood up from our seats halfway across the room and headed over to McGwire's table.

"Excuse me, Mr. McGwire," I started out politely. "My friend Laine would love—"

"Can't you see I'm with friends," the fan-favorite abruptly interrupted me in the harshest tone. His voice continued to rise. "What the fuck do you want?"

I just stared back and calmly told him in an eerily quiet voice, "Nothing. Nothing at all." I turned around and walked back to my friends.

I get it. Famous people can't just go to dinner and enjoy a nice evening out without being bothered by the likes of little ole me. It's understandable. They just want some normalcy in life without being hounded every second by random people who don't know them. On the other hand, Mark McGwire was being paid millions to hit a little Rawlings stitched white ball over a fence.

McGwire wasn't teaching kids. He didn't know how to perform life-saving surgery. He hadn't discovered a new cure for cancer. He played baseball. And as a result, even after cheating his way to the top, he's still worth over sixty million for that earthshattering talent. Wasn't being recognized for his fame in exchange for being approached by fans a fair trade for getting rich off of playing with a ball? "Trust me, Laine, you don't want to meet him," I told my friend back at our table.

Not all athletes act like that. When I was at a legal conference at the Ritz Carlton in Key Biscayne, Florida in the spring of 2009, I had a different experience. I had just returned to the hotel after a night out. It was late. Like one in the morning. I sat in the lobby for a few minutes when a large black Escalade pulled up to the valet area you could see through the open front doors. Out stepped NBA legend Magic Johnson. He was a lot larger than I had imagined him, mostly because the Magic I knew was from watching him, Dr. J, Larry Bird and the like as a kid.

He also had put on quite a bit of weight since those days. When he walked into the hotel, Magic was all smiles. And I mean genuine smiles. Hello to the bell hop. Hellos to the front desk people. He even waved over to me just to be friendly. A true gentleman. I walked over and we chatted for a few moments. Nothing important. But I knew my boys, who were only ages six and four at the time, would be excited to hear about it. They always get excited when I meet famous people, but especially athletes. That's partially my fault, partially society's.

Actor George Clooney was also the complete opposite of Mark McGwire. My friend Sam's brother owned a long vacant large building in downtown St. Louis. The modern architectural gem, the GenAm Building. General American Life Insurance Company had its national headquarters there but left in 2004, and the building had remained vacant for a good decade.

In 2008, DreamWorks decided to rent the building to film its movie *Up in the Air*. The movie was about a corporate downsizer (played by George Clooney) who flew around the country firing workers. Anna Kendrick was Clooney's co-star. Sam graciously told me if I ever wanted to watch any of the filming, I could come. I immediately jumped at the opportunity. Within days, I was watching Clooney and Kendrick filming one of the scenes. After about an hour of filming one particular five-minute scene, I decided to introduce myself to Clooney. I walked into the middle of the set where he was seated.

"Good morning, Mr. Clooney. I love your work.," I said to him with a smile. He looked me straight in the eye and reached out his hand. "Good morning. What's your name," he responded as we shook hands. "I'm Jeffrey Kass. Fantastic meeting you." He smiled warmly and just said "you too, Jeffrey." Now here's the thing. I'm straight. No exception. I like women. But Clooney was so strikingly handsome, I later joked with my friend Joe that I'd even date him. I think Joe once joked the same thing about Adam Levine when we passed an advertisement for Maroon 5 at a mall in Atlanta.

As I was walking away from Clooney, I turned around and said "by the way, when you're done filming, please get the hell out of St. Louis. No way any of us guys can compete with you here." He chuckled, but I sensed it wasn't the first time he'd heard that. I would've introduced myself to Anna Kendrick, too, but she was overly engaged in an intense texting back and forth and wasn't very approachable, not that such vibes had stopped me in the past.

My brief but pleasant interaction with Clooney was somewhat similar to an encounter I had in 2001 while visiting Los Angeles for work. I found my way to Beverly Hills, mostly because I've always loved good fashion and wanted to window shop. I couldn't exactly afford Christian Dior or Valentino yet, but I still loved to look and dream. The one place I could afford in that neighborhood was a chocolate shop a street or two over from Rodeo Drive. Edelweiss Chocolates. I'm not sure if it's still there, and I probably couldn't find it on a map today. But when I walked into the store in 2001, Reese Witherspoon was leaning over the glass case right in front of me, eyeing the fancy chocolate offerings.

She heard me come in and briefly turned and smiled. To be honest, she just looked like a normal person. Sure, she was put together, but had I not seen *Legally Blonde* two months prior I may not have even recognized her without all that Hollywood makeup. That definitely changes a person's look. "Hey, how's your day?" I said to her as our mouths both watered over the gourmet treats. "It's great!" she said with her now famous smile. "Are you enjoying this sunshine?" she asked as I noticed she actually had a slight Southern accent. It was small talk for sure, but Witherspoon was just a normal nice person, not at all bothered by my presence. We exchanged a laugh over our mutual chocolate addiction and went on with our day.

When former Ohio State national championship running back Maurice Clarett visited the alumni club in Denver a few years ago, I would've figured he'd be humble after ruining his career and serving time in prison for weapons and other charges. No such luck. I've always been a second chance kind of guy, so I reached out my hand to introduce myself and he brushed me off like a mosquito. No handshake. Just looked directly at me and said nothing. I walked away. I wasn't that excited to meet him anyway, but I had hoped he learned a lesson and was traveling around to promote how he's improved his life. Nope. Just another macho cocky athlete.

My experience trying to meet Eddie Murphy in high school wasn't much different. My friends Joel, Sam, and I scored backstage passes after Murphy's 1986 *Pieces of My Mind* concert. It was the same set for the movie *Raw*. Anyone who was a teenager in 1982 knew Eddie Murphy was the funniest man on earth. We all memorized every joke from his *Delirious* concert album. So when we headed up the elevators at the Hyatt in downtown Columbus to cash in our backstage passes, you can imagine how excited we were.

We arrived at his suite on the eighth floor and knocked. A large body bouncer cracked open the door and greeted us in an unwelcoming stern voice. "Can I help you?" As I held out my backstage pass, I could hear girls giggling inside the suite. I peeked through the door and could see Murphy in some red leather jacket. Murphy uttered a few words to the bouncer, the last of which were "get 'em outta here." The bouncer physically pushed me away from the door, looked at our seventeen-year-old selves and just shook his head back and forth. "Sorry, sorry, you can't come in. This is for adults." And then he abruptly shut the door.

Before the Eddie Murphy debacle, my first famous encounter I had was with the '80s band REO Speedwagon. One of my many teenage jobs was working at the concert hall at the Ohio Center in downtown Columbus right at the corner of High Street and Nationwide Boulevard. The benefit of working as an usher at concerts was that I got to go backstage at every show in the short three months I worked there. The Fabulous Thunderbirds. WWF wrestlers. Quiet Riot. REO Speedwagon was the most memorable, though. Lead singer Kevin Cronin was so warm and friendly, and even told me he loved my funky sunglasses.

I also met golfers Fuzzy Zoeller and Fred Couples in high school, as well as major league baseball hall of famer Johnny Bench. Fuzzy was funny. Fred was an ass. Johnny Bench was friendly.

In 2019, I attended a KRS-One concert. KRS-One, who led the rap group Boogie Down Productions in the late eighties and nineties, was my favorite rapper of all time. I started listening to him in the spring of 1987, the end of my senior year of high school. For you white folks who've never heard of him, he raps about political stuff, philosophy, history, and other important things. Probably why he never really hit the mainstream, although his song "Jack of Spades" was the theme song for the well-known movie *New Jack City* in 1991. I loved most rap back then. Eric B. and Rakim, Big Daddy Kane, Run DMC, The Beastie Boys, Tribe Called Quest, De La Soul and some lesser known but spectacular groups like The Goats, Blood of Abraham, and 7A3.

I still have all their cassettes and records, although my girl-friend has been hounding me to downsize. "Why do you need to keep this stuff?" I just can't let go. KRS-One was the best of the rappers. I hadn't seen him in concert in over twenty years, so when I found out he was coming to Denver I immediately bought tickets. He was just an early twenties-something kid when he hit the scene in 1987, but in 2019, he was already in his fifties. I wondered how he would be, but he didn't disappoint.

He rapped his classics, did some poetry, and even threw in some newer political songs. Simply an amazing concert.

The concert ended at about one in the morning, and I saw a short line of people behind a rope ready to go backstage. I didn't have backstage tickets, but I still moseyed my way over to the line. There was a middle-aged Black woman with gray hair holding a clipboard. She looked like the one in charge. I excused myself around the small crowd and said hello to her.

"I know the answer probably is no, but I've loved his music for over thirty years. His music inspired me to a life of fighting bigotry. I even took Black Studies in college in part because of his lyrics. Is there any chance you could let me backstage to meet him?" I asked with a sorta puppy dog look on my face. I wasn't expecting it to work and sure enough she politely responded with a no. "Sorry, I can't do that." I headed toward the exit of the concert venue, head slightly down. Then she came running over. "Oh, damnit! Get over here. Now I feel guilty. I'll let you back."

About a half hour later, now approaching one forty-five in the morning, she let the group of about eight of us backstage. There he was, a towering six-foot four KRS-One with short dreads, standing there ready to give us a philosophy lesson. After we all got to give him an embrace and introduce ourselves, KRS-One began discussing how we have the opportunity right now to manifest where we want life to be in twenty years. He believed he manifested the moment we were in at some point. I was touched when he reflected on how he was sleeping homeless on a bench in New York and then years later performed at a venue located at the very same spot as the bench.

"I manifested that moment while I was homeless," he remarked. At one point, noticing it was now two-thirty in the morning and well past my fifty-year-old body's bedtime, I chimed in. "Well, if we're going to manifest where we'll be in twenty years when we are in our seventies, can we start that concert at three p.m.?" KRS-One laughed and pointed to me. "You got it, brother," he smiled, still giggling.

Maybe all rappers are just cool. When on vacation in Amsterdam with my kids in 2019, I walked into the lobby of our hotel and Chuck D of Public Enemy was standing right there. He was so warm and friendly and we even half-joked about how I refused to listen to the group when rapper Professor Griff was a part of it back in the nineties. "I couldn't handle it because he didn't like us Jews so much," I told Chuck D. "You weren't alone. There were a lot of people who had problems with him," he quickly acknowledged, laughing back.

We chatted for a while, along with co-band member James Bomb. They were just normal down-to-earth people, although when I later connected with them on social media, James Bomb turned out to be a big promoter of notorious anti-Semite Louis Farrakhan and The Nation of Islam. Bruce Springstein's E Street member Steven Van Zandt was at the Amsterdam hotel, too, but I wasn't a fan of most Rock-n-Roll so I just smiled and continued on my way. I mean, I like The Beatles and maybe some Rolling Stones, but never really got into most other Rock.

I got to meet reggae rap folk singer Matisyahu twice. Once at a Jewish Sabbath Friday night dinner in St. Louis sometime in 2005 or 2006, and once backstage at a concert in Boulder in 2014. He was quiet at the dinner, and the backstage experience didn't go well. He was so high he could barely complete a sentence. It didn't surprise me since he barely could sing lyrics to some of his more popular songs an hour prior. Shit, I even knew the lyrics better. He must've cleaned up since because his last concert in Denver was spectacular, but I still want my seventy-five dollars back from the Boulder performance.

I almost decided to leave out all the stories of famous national stage politicians` I met since they all have a reason to be friendly. They probably act more than real actors most of the time if we're being honest, but I'd like to think I'm good at weeding out the fakers anyway.

I met George W. Bush when he visited St. Louis a few years after 9/11. Solid, friendly, warm. All-around good guy. He had a goofy smile and laugh, but they were authentic and disarming. I tried telling my liberal friends to stop calling him the devil over policy disagreements because someday you'd get the devil and see the difference. That was long before I ever imagined Trump. Prophetic or just bad luck? It turns out Bush wasn't the most effective president we ever had, and I'm not here to whitewash thousands who died for the bullshit Iraq war, but you could tell his heart was in it.

I met Bill Clinton in Toledo, Ohio when he was campaigning for president in 1992. It felt like a John Kennedy moment for me and had it not been for all the incessant infidelity stuff that came out later, I may have washed my hands after shaking his. I was in law school at the time and quite ideological. Still am, but maybe with a dose of maturity and realism now.

Bill was so charming. Looked you right in the eye as he shook your hand with another hand on your shoulder. Made you feel like you were the only person in the room for that two seconds. One right-wing journalist at the time even quipped that if Bill Clinton could shake every American's hand, he'd win ninety percent of the vote. It sure worked on me, although with my own dad's infidelity as a kid, I could never really idolize Bill no matter how good his policies were. Too triggering. My friend Keith took a bunch of pictures of the moment with me and Bill, but unfortunately Keith's fingers dominated the photographs more than the future president.

Four years prior, I met 1988 Democratic presidential candidate Mike Dukakis at Ohio State. He got into an elevator with me, and when the top of his just over five-foot-six frame came up to my eyes, I instinctively knew there was no way this guy was going to be president and beat the six-foot-two George H.W. Bush. I'm sure Dukakis's larger-than-life bushy eyebrows didn't help either. Not that eyebrows should matter or that short people shouldn't be president, but we as a country seem to have this picture of a tall strong man as our leader. Total bullshit if you ask me, and not just because I'm five foot eight and shrinking, but that was the reality at the time. Sure enough, Dukakis lost to the less dynamic Bush. And you think we have problems electing a woman!

One of my favorite exchanges was with Senator John McCain a few years ago. I was walking to my gate at Denver International Airport sometime in 2015 and John McCain had just exited his plane and headed in my direction. He had a distinct look, so he was easy to spot. I stopped to say hello. "Good afternoon Senator McCain. I just wanted to tell you as a Jewish American how much I appreciate your support for Israel over the years." McCain didn't pause. "It's the right thing to do," was his blunt response. "Well," I continued, "I sure hope your party finds its way back to the middle." "You and me both," he responded as he graciously shook my hand and continued on his way.

Over the years I've met a dozen or so other senators and governors, and another twenty or so Congressmen. Democrats, Republicans. John Kasich. Kit Bond. John Danforth. Howard Metzenbaum. Sherrod Brown. John Hickenlooper. Michael

Bennett. Mark Udall. Many more. All relatively polished, nice, respectful. The way you want your politicians to be for the most part.

The most impressive of the politicians I met, though, was Barack Obama. Not President Obama, but the mostly unknown Illinois state Senator Obama, who in 2004 was running for the U.S. Senate seat in Illinois. He was in St. Louis for a fundraiser and my friend Rick asked if I wanted to attend. I had never heard of the guy but decided to go nonetheless. "I heard this guy is the real deal," Rick coaxed me. The cost of admission was only one hundred dollars so I agreed to go. The event was at the relatively new Westin Hotel in downtown St. Louis. There were only about fifty or so people in a small conference room, and only three of us were white and I think one worked at the hotel. Mr. Obama walked in without any bodyguards with his signature smile and shook a few hands, mine one of them, before he found his way to the front of the room.

His speech was about how we engage in disagreement in this country, admonishing the mostly Black audience that someone's idea isn't wrong just because it comes from the other side of the political spectrum. He asked us to try to understand another's feelings about an issue. "If someone thinks abortion is murder," Obama began as an example, "then it's understandable why they might think someone who wants that to be legal is way off base. If someone in Southern Illinois went hunting with their family for generations, and they feared you might take away their guns, you should understand why they might oppose you."

Although he then joked how he once told a Southern Illinois gun owner, "Why do you need a semiautomatic weapon? Can't you give the deer a running chance?" Obama gave example after example of how we can do a better job of understanding each other even if we can't always agree. His speech was about bringing a new approach to Washington. One where we listen to each other and treat each other respectfully. I'm sure he couldn't have imagined the absurd level of abuse and hatred he was going to later experience while president, but you could tell his heart and goals were in the right place.

The really cool thing about the Obama fundraiser was that I got to have a semiprivate audience with him after the event ended. I talked to Obama about race issues and Israel for a good ten minutes. You could tell he was internally balancing his very strong and unwavering belief in a secure and forever lasting Jewish homeland with his desire for Palestinians to also have their own country. It was sincere and heartfelt, regardless of how the media portrayed him on the topic over the next decade.

I'm not a prophet, but one thing was obvious to me after listening to Obama. So I blurted out my thoughts to him during our exchange about Israel. "I know you're going to be president someday. When that happens, please don't forget about the specialness of our friendship with Israel." "I won't," he said back without hesitation or political qualification. This was the first time in my life where I believed we could have a Black president. Rick, who is Black, thought I was on crack.

When I moved to Denver in 2011 so my ex-wife could get remarried to a guy she met there, I jokingly threatened her then fiancé, "Hey, if I agree to move to Colorado, I get your Lakers tickets." Her soon to be husband shared part of a season ticket package to the Denver Nuggets. Courtside seats right behind the scorer's table where the players would check in before entering the game. Well, I agreed to move, not for Lakers tickets but to show cooperation and kindness as a lesson for my kids and so their mom could find happiness again.

Still, her husband gave me the tickets anyway. February 2, 2012. Lakers versus Nuggets. Pepsi Center. There I was, sitting just feet away from the two teams. The Nuggets to my right. The Lakers a little further down my left. One of my all-time favorite players, Kobe Bryant, who was at the tail end of his career, was checking back into the game during the second quarter. Now just eight feet away from me. "Hey Kobe!! So fun to see you play here in Denver," and then I reached out my hand to fist pump him. He turned, looked at me and smiled, then fist pumped me back. I still wanted the Lakers to lose, but my four-second exchange with one of the greatest players of all time made my night despite the Nuggets losing 93 to 89.

It turns out, all these famous people are just a bunch of damn humans after all. Tall, short, Black, white, skinny, fat, mean, kind, indifferent, caring, funny, boring. Assholes, dickheads, generous people, amazing people. You know, just like the rest of us.

Rona Day 69

We really need a leader, not a tweeter.

Rona Day 70: Take a Knee

Corona has taken a back seat as we are now in day five of major unrest in this country over the murder of George Floyd by Minneapolis police.

The violence, destruction, and looting have sadly overshadowed the killing of Floyd.

Lots of social media posts by white folks expressing outrage over the violence. Justified but shallow nonetheless. It dawned on me that a lot of these same people ridiculed a certain Super Bowl quarterback when he peacefully took a knee in protest over repetitive police killing of unarmed Black men.

I think you have the message now, Black people. Don't express your anger violently and don't express it peacefully. Just keep your mouth shut.

How about this instead. Why don't we get outraged at the pervasive and systemic racism in this country? Then a knee and an afro won't seem so offensive.

In between kites and lightning, Ben Franklin said it best: "Justice will not be served until those unaffected are as outraged as those who are."

I'm not a fan of violence, but maybe the fear of destruction and looting will end white silence once and for all.

Rona Day 71

There was a very wealthy Jewish businessman in England in the nineteenth century. Sir Moses Montefiore. When he was old and frail, a person boldly asked him what his worth was. "Name me a number," the admirer asked. "Surely, with all your stocks, bonds, and investments, it must be high." He pondered the question and responded that his worth was not contained on any balance sheets. "It's in the poor person's hand. The orphan's home. The widow's oven. It's in the schools and villages where I emptied my pockets. If you want to know my worth, add all of those up and you will get a number."

It's time we look at our own privileges and places in life and use that success and influence to empty our own pockets to repair a country in need of intense healing.

Rona Day 72: Cornhole

ESPN has officially run out of recorded games to play. By my count, the Bulls have now won eighty-six NBA championships if we tally up how many times their games have been rebroadcast during Corona. The other day, ESPN aired the national cornhole championships, with competitors wearing Corona masks. I mean, I miss sports, but seriously? Cornhole championships? What's next, redneck golf? You know where you toss those ropes with golf balls attached to each end and try to have them wrap around short beams. How about Monopoly competitions? Or Risk? What if football, basketball, and baseball never come back and we're stuck with Wheaties boxes featuring the world Euchre champion? Will there be a cornhole all-star game?

Rona Day 73

It almost sounds like everyone is speaking in dog these days, trying to order coffee through a mask. "Rerro. Row are ru?"

I think the woman in front of me was trying to order an oat milk coffee, but instead the barista repeated back the request, "You want a whole milk latte?" To be fair, what she really asked for was a "roat milk ratte."

Rona Day 75: Kike

Corona forced us home with nothing to do. No concerts. No trips. No sports. We hall had to just pay attention to what was happening around us. Kids. Partners. Home projects. And yes, racism. Ahmaud Arbery. Christian Cooper. George Floyd. But let's face it. These were just the soups du jour. The problems persisted for years. We were just too absorbed in our wine tasting parties to notice.

While I won't ever know what it's like to live in Black or brown skin, I've known about hatred and bigotry walking the planet as a Jewish man. My first rude awakening was in 1987, during my freshman year at Ohio State in my dormitory, Steeb Hall. The dorm is located on the south end of the Ohio State campus, along with several others. It was the more desirable part of campus, for freshmen at least, because all the good college bars were located within four minutes' walking distance.

Mean Mr. Mustard's was the alternative music bar on the corner of eleventh and High Street. It's where I learned about tattoos, pink hair, and something called slam dancing, where kids would literally ram into each other on the dance floor. I've never been one for pain, so just one try was enough for me. Mother Fletcher's was next door and played a mix of alternative and Top 40. You had to walk down a long flight of steps to get to the underground bar, which seemed mysterious to a college student.; except I had already snuck in several times in high school, so it wasn't that cool to me anymore.

Two doors down, you had Park Alley, which was more or less a frat Top 40 dance bar. Not an uncommon sight to see drunk, rich white kids vomiting on their way out at two in the morning at Papa Joe's, a two-story bar across the street. It basically was a loud, sit-down, beer-guzzling bar, which I only visited once or twice for "kegs and eggs" before Buckeye football games Saturday mornings. The juicy rumor about that place was that some inebriated college senior fell over the balcony to the first floor and was hospitalized.

Not only were students in bar heaven on this part of campus, there was a Buffalo Wild Wings (back then called BW3s), a one-dollar gyro joint, and something called All-In-One that served Taco Bell, Pizza Hut, and KFC all under one roof, providing plenty of fuel for my freshman fifteen. Another four or five bars I never even ventured into were also nearby, but I can't recall their names now since some greedy real estate developers demolished all these places well after I graduated in favor of drab retail, an Aveda salon, a high-end sports bar, and T-Mobile. Prior to the so-called beautification of High Street, Ohio State probably had more bars per square foot than anywhere else in the country. Needless to say, I felt like I had hit the jackpot when I got my first-year dorm assignment in 1987.

Most of the other dorms were on the north side of campus, and it took students a good twenty to thirty minutes to walk to the cool south-end bars on weekends. Kids in those dorms sometimes even took campus buses to the south side it was so far. Two other twenty-six story dorms were located even further away near Ohio Stadium along the Olentangy River, referred to us back then as the Olengrungy since it wasn't the most pleasant or clean river one ever saw. Brown and muddy to match the all-too-frequent gray skies of Columbus, Ohio.

I was definitely grateful I hadn't been assigned to either of the two lone towers, named Morrill and Lincoln. Legend had it that Ohio State built one of these towers for every virgin to graduate since Ohio State was founded in 1870. That's a grand total of two virgin graduates in over one hundred years! It certainly made me feel good about my odds of meeting girls.

My dorm, however geographically desirable, was a total culture shock to me. I had gone to high school with a fair mix of people. Most of my close friends as a teenager were either Jewish or Black. Even a few kids from Yugoslavia and a Native American boy. But Steeb Hall was different. I was the only Jew on the eighth floor in a sea of white kids from mostly small-town Ohio. Sean from Massillon. Corey from Marietta. Luke from Lima, just to name a few. The only good thing about my floor was that it was co-ed, and the girls from rural Ohio were just as pretty as the rest of them. Sometimes even better, although my dry, curly, nappy, untamed Jewfro wasn't exactly a turn-on to this demographic. Hell, I *know* it wasn't a turn-on for anyone. Thank God I later discovered hair gel after law school.

My roommates were Len from Berea, a mostly white and conservative suburb on the west side of Cleveland, and Billy from mostly rural Mansfield, Ohio. Len was a quiet kid. He knew a ton about sports but didn't talk about much else. Nice enough guy, but he decided to pledge the Tau Kappa Epsilon fraternity that first fall semester, so I rarely saw him. Tekes, as his frat brothers were called, boasted Ronald Reagan as one of their alumni.

Billy wasn't as docile as Len. Opinionated. Loud. And full-on redneck. He was tall, maybe six-foot four. Had a lanky frame. Albino blonde Aryan-like hair with hazel eyes and lots of freckles. Always cracking jokes, except their frequency about race and homosexuality irritated me. Still, he never really bothered me personally. Even asked me to pitch on his intramural softball team since I had played for my Jewish youth group team in high school. Billy high-fived me after good plays from time to time. I'm sure I could've fared worse than Len and Billy.

In 1987, Ohio State had about fifty thousand undergraduate students, but my new life was more about the forty or so kids on my dorm floor—most of whom never met a nice Jewish boy, or any Jewish boy for that matter.

"Wait, so you guys don't believe in Jesus?" a well-meaning girl Cara from Findley, Ohio asked me just before our first all-floor dorm meeting the day before classes started. It hadn't taken long for the entire floor to discover I was Jewish. I wore it like a badge of honor, so it wasn't exactly a secret. Cara wasn't trying to be abrasive, but her tone suggested a level of *how in the fuck is that even possible you don't believe in Jesus* approach to the subject. I had never been asked this type of question before and was almost scared to let her in on the dirty truth of what us Jews believe. "Well, um . . . no . . . We just think Jesus was a really good person," I responded apologetically, although I actually had no idea whether Judaism thought Jesus was cool—especially since so many of my ancestors were killed in the name of Jesus over the years.

Our synagogue in Columbus, Temple Israel, certainly wasn't discussing Jesus. We were too busy learning about the names of death camps in Poland and Germany to be bothered with belief systems. I knew about Auschwitz and Buchenwald long before I ever heard the words Genesis and Leviticus. You can imagine the joys of that education. "Good morning boys and girls! You're Jewish! So guess what? Your brothers and sisters were gassed by the Germans!" All I really knew about Jesus was from having to watch my childhood neighbor Billy perform in *Passion of the Christ* plays at his church when I was nine. I got the pleasure of watching child actors playing my co-religionists rat out poor Jesus, leading him to his demise.

My first semester at Ohio State consisted of Business Calculus, Hebrew 101, Physics, and Black Studies 101. A full class load. Ohio State required students to take four semesters of a foreign language, so I signed up for Hebrew. I had a bar mitzvah at age thirteen and figured I would coast through with straight As. That idea lasted for one semester, and I ended up dropping Hebrew before my freshman year was over. I didn't sign up for Hebrew so I would actually have to study! Damn that language was hard. I really didn't appreciate what Black Studies was either, but since I had a lot of Black friends, I signed up with two friends from high school who were also attending Ohio State.

The Black Studies course was a welcome respite from my whitewashed dorm floor. Nobody looked at me like the odd man out, despite being only one of two white kids in class. The other one, Emily, was dating one of the football players, and before the world of cell phones and text messages, spent more time passing notes to her boyfriend than asking about West African history. Still, nobody there questioned my presence in class.

The problem with the course, though, was that it made life more stressful by opening my eyes to society's black-white divide. Up until this point, I thought racism was a 1960s thing. My fifty-fifty mixed Black-white high school seemed uneventful. Friendships with Black kids were organic and natural. So when our instructor began discussing the rampant and pervasive racism in society, I was stunned. When students one after the other shared their horrific experiences, it made me angry. And I mean really angry. I had to take that anger back with me to my *The Dukes of Hazzard* dorm and navigate my evolving feelings every day.

The kids in my dorm were by no means card-carrying members of the KKK or intentionally racist. But their all-white worldview stood in stark contrast from what I was learning in Black Studies. I felt as though I was living in two separate countries. This was the first time I had actually even realized I was white myself. I always thought being Jewish was a separate race until I heard the almost daily trauma of what people of color endure. Yes, I knew I was different from the other white students; but let's not kid ourselves, I still got to go to a bank and, despite my Eastern-European Jewish hair, get serviced without incident.

The first time I became aware of my own skin color, which I like to exotically call *olive,* although I never actually ate an olive that looked like me, was in my third week of college. The kid next to me in Black Studies was Tommy. He was from University Heights, in Cleveland, a mixed Jewish and Black neighborhood. Darker than most Black kids I knew. Short and a little pudgy. A shaved head. Always joking around with a smile. "What up white boy Kassanova," he greeted me one morning with a warm clasp of our right hands, making a play on my last name, Kass. White boy? What was he talking about? I actually looked at the back of my hand to check myself out. Was I really white? Should I be offended? I thought I was Jewish, not white, but alas Crayola never added the color "Jewish" to the box of sixty-four.

Over the next few weeks, I couldn't stop thinking that maybe I was just like all the other white kids on the eighth floor of Steeb Hall. I mean, other than one kid in high school who was a bit crazy anyway and seemed to hate all groups, I never experienced any hatred because of my Jewish identity. Certainly nothing directed at me. It had been relatively smooth sailing for me, which stood in clear contrast to my Black Studies classmates' lives. Despite my dad's never-ending admonishment against anti-Semites my entire childhood, I hadn't actually met one and figured he was just stuck as a victim of another era. I wasn't completely ignorant. I read about how Jews were excluded from clubs, universities and the like. I read about Jews being called kikes. But all that seemed a thing of the past relegated now to just a few nut cases like Louis Farrakhan, Pat Robertson, or Lyndon LaRouche.

You can imagine, then, how utterly stunned I was when I arrived at my dorm room at 2:35 p.m. on Wednesday, October 21, 1987 to a giant three-foot by three-foot red swastika painted on the door. It was so big it almost covered the entire top half of the door to our room. At least that's how I remember it. I suppose any size swastika would seem big to me. The red paint was the same color hue the Nazis used in their flag, which before then I only saw in history books. I stood there shaking but also in some sort of this-isn't-really-happening frozen shock. By the time I was in law school five years later and saw "Die Jews" painted on the walls of the elevator at the University of Toledo College of Law, I was used to the hatred, but at a naïve eighteen years old, tears began flowing down my face as Len opened the door.

"That thing was on there when I got back an hour ago," he said stoically, as it became apparent that he hadn't shared his discovery with anyone yet.

That thing? I said nothing in response and instead called the campus police.

"Ohio State Campus Emergency," the woman answered the phone after I dialed 0, years before 911 existed.

"Yes, I was just the victim of an anti-Semitic incident. A Nazi symbol was painted on my door in Steeb Hall, room 801," I told the operator.

"I'm so sorry, we'll send someone over right away," the woman on the other end of the phone said back. I couldn't tell if she was really sorry or not.

Fifteen minutes later, two of Ohio State's finest showed up in uniform.

"Is this the only thing that happened," one of the officers asked me as his opening question. I gave him a bewildered look.

"What do you mean, only? Yes, this is what happened," I told him as more tears flowed down the sides of my cheeks.

"Listen, son," as he put his arm on my shoulder. "People just use that symbol as graffiti all the time and it doesn't mean you were targeted because you're Jewish."

I couldn't believe my ears as I reminded him "But … I'm the only Jewish kid on the floor and my door is the only one with the swastika."

The second officer backed his partner up. "You realize the symbol actually was originally from India and it had nothing to do with the Nazis."

I hadn't ever heard that one before, although I've since learned his bullshit explanation is technically true. Not sure why this cop knew that info, but okay. Over the years, I've come to realize that's the same refrain repeated by anti-Semites and their silent supporters. My teenage self knew the cop's response was absurd, but I didn't have enough life experience yet to let the depth of his ignorant comment sink in.

It wasn't just Len who hadn't reported the incident. None of the other kids who saw the paint before me did either. Even after a dozen or so of them watched my tears as the police questioned me in the hallway did one so much as say an "I'm sorry" or "how awful." They just stood and stared like they were watching a building burn to the ground. A nauseating combination of disbelief and a how-cool-is-that curiosity on their faces. Most of them couldn't even look at me after I called the police, with one kid Vince rhetorically asking me the next day, "You didn't think the police would actually do anything, did you? It was just paint." I was angry yet felt sorry for the lot of them. Their world was filled with ignorance and a certain narrowness that might never allow them to truly experience the beauty of other types of people.

It wasn't enough that my eighteen-year-old world was just shattered with red paint strokes on my door, but the police weren't taking this seriously on top of it? Maybe Dad was right all along. Maybe the entire world still hated us Jews like they had for the past three thousand years. College students. The police. Everyone. Maybe I would've been more prepared for this had I listened to Dad. I just couldn't accept a world that hated me. How depressing. How stressful that must be for any group that endures regular hatred, I thought then and know now. No wonder we Jews are Tums' best customers. I used to think the pervasive stomach problems many Jews experience was just a result of unhealthy Jewish food, but I wouldn't be surprised if generations of hate-induced stress creeped into the Jewish gene pool and that's just how we're wired now.

The next two days were a whirlwind. I couldn't sleep. I couldn't focus on classes. I started suspecting at least three people on my floor as possible perpetrators. My main suspect was my roommate Billy. His softball high-fives weren't enough to render his racial jokes insignificant. He just looked and acted like the Webster's Dictionary definition of redneck. Without the help of the police, though, I knew I'd never figure out who the budding racist door artist was. So instead of fighting, standing up for myself, or letting people know I wouldn't take it—all reasonable choices—I let fear win.

I rushed to the Ohio State dorm assignment office and quickly got permission to move dorms to Morrill Tower, that virgin dorm all the way on the northwest side of campus, about as far away from the south campus bars as one could imagine. And far away from the Hitler youth in Steeb Hall. I would never have to see those powder white faces again, and I didn't for my remaining four years of college. Not once did I run into Len, Billy, Cara, or any of my other dorm mates on Ohio State's vast 1,700-acre campus.

Dad reported the incident to the office of Ohio State President Ed Jennings, but they did nothing, just like the police. ABC news anchor Peter Jennings, the president's brother, was known to report negatively lopsided on Israel quite regularly, so I wasn't surprised by the idea that paid no small part in his brother's inaction.

The only person at Ohio State who shared any sympathy about the hate crime other than the student housing office was Mr. Thompson. He was the sixty-something-year-old Black maintenance man who was tasked by the university with removing the blood-colored paint from my door. "Man, that's fucked up. Do they know who did it?" he asked me with a disgusted yet comforting look. He was the first person who calmed me down for at least a few moments. Not because he all of a sudden made me feel safe or because what happened wasn't as bad as I thought, but because of the empathy in his eyes. He undoubtedly had endured years of racism trumping my swastika experience and knew what it must feel like to come face to face with hatred.

"The police aren't even trying to catch the person," I responded. "Typical," he said, disgusted, and looked at me again with understanding even though we hadn't engaged in a full discussion. I stood there watching him erase the rank hatred from my door with some ammonia smelling chemicals. Usually strong smells like that cause me to gag, but this time I was unaffected, lost in my thoughts about our shared experience.

Campus housing helped me gather my things and move dorms a few days later. My new dorm room, on the seventeenth floor, was more like the United Nations rather than a random sample of ten of Ohio's eighty-eight cornfield counties. A Pakistani kid. Three Black kids. A girl from Chile. One Jewish girl from Chicago, who unfortunately wasn't my type. A New Yorker. Someone from Houston. And one Chinese student. Despite my newfound happy place, I was still angry. Sure, I was still pissed some asshole painted a swastika on my door, but angrier at myself for not fighting back. For not clenching my fists and letting people know that if they messed with my five-six frame, I was gonna give it to them. (I'm glad I grew another three inches in college.)

I couldn't believe I moved dorms. "What the fuck was I thinking?" I thought to myself for weeks on end. That anti-Semite who did this was probably laughing at me. I'm sure he thought us Jews must be a bunch of pocket-protector pussies, like the media often portrays us. Accountants. Stockbrokers. Nerds. But not Navy SEALs or prize fighters. The truth is that Jews actually make up about two percent of the military and two percent of the general population in the U.S., and Jews actually dominated boxing in the 1920s until places like Harvard ended their Jewish quota system. Hardly just a bunch of nerds. Sixty years later though, we're just a bunch of pushovers to most people. My walking away from Steeb with my head down only confirmed that idea.

My anger took over. I decided I was no longer going to stand for hatred of any kind. I didn't care if it came from Arabs against Jews. Jews against Arabs. Whites against Blacks. Anti-gay. Anything. My eyes were going to remain open. I was going to be "woke," as they call it today. I was fucking done with hatred. I was determined to stomp it out. To shout it down. Nobody was ever going to run me out of my home again.

I started organizing protests for race issues I read about in the news or for incidents that happened on campus. One involved police abuse of an unarmed Black kid. Yes, that shit was happening even twenty-five years ago. It was easy to protest the police after how they treated my situation. I protested the school's newspaper the *Lantern* when they published a Holocaust denier's advertisement in the name of free speech, although I'm pretty sure the U.S. Constitution didn't require them to run the paid ad. I started working on political campaigns. I wasn't just protesting and working on issues, I was doing so with fire in my eyes. As far as I was concerned, every regular white guy was a racist. It was easy to fill my cup with anger, too, when my circle of friends consisted mostly of Jews and Black people.

My four, okay let's call it five, years at Ohio State were a flurry of nonstop political activity and fighting racism. Everything flowed from that. The courses I took. My efforts. It became my reason for living.

The problem, though, was of course not all regular white people are consciously racist. Not even all white Republicans are racist. It hit me hard in the face in law school when I met Mark Gross. Mark was a blonde kid of German descent. German last name. German face. German hair and eyes. He looked and smelled German. Like he just ate a few bratwursts and drank some Bavarian-style beer. So when he met me and started with a "You don't look Jewish" comment, I lost it.

"What the fuck is that supposed to mean," I responded in a high-pitched voice, my swastika anger still hot in my belly. "Do Ethiopian Jews look Jewish? Do Mexican Jews look Jewish? How about Swiss Jews? What are we supposed to look like?" My tone was aggressive. The funny thing about the incident was that I actually do look European Jewish, minus the stereotypical large Jewish nose. "Whoa. Slow down," Mark said in a state of disbelief. "I didn't mean anything negative about it." Mark was visibly shaken by my unwelcome reprimand. I knew nothing about Mark, and here I was basically accusing him of being racist.

It later turned out that Mark was from a small town of only two thousand people in Ohio. Strident, conservative, religious Republican. Anti–gay marriage. Anti–affirmative action. Anti-abortion. Straight down the line far-right wing. But despite abhorring many of Mark's political views, I quickly realized at best he didn't know better from his upbringing and at worst he was just repeating stereotypes about the "Jewish look." Mark wasn't a Jew hater. He wasn't out to put me down. To the contrary, he would go on to ask my help on various law school subjects and always showed me respect as a fellow human being the rest of my three years of law school.

Mark was the bucket of water I needed dumped over my narrow head to put out some of the overreaching anger still lingering from my run-in with Nazi art. And just in the nick of time before I left law school to interact with the rest of society, which lo and behold is mostly white and Christian. Mark unintentionally balanced me out. To distinguish between real racism and ignorance. To intelligently react to situations differently based on the motivation of the actor. It wasn't that I stopped hating hatred. Or that racism was okay so long as it came in an unintentional form. It's just that everyone has a story, a background, an upbringing—and if I was going to be part of society's solution, I needed to stop my own racial profiling. I needed to know when to speak up and when to keep quiet and process instead.

I had the pleasure of having dinner with civil rights activist Dr. Cornell West in 2018. Dr. West has been one of the seminal voices and philosophers on race issues in America for the last thirty-plus years. He teaches at Harvard and Princeton and travels the U.S. fighting racism. We were discussing, what else, various racial issues when Dr. West reminded me of a hope that gets lost in the battle for racial justice. "My dear Jewish brother Jeffrey," Dr. West began in his typically warm manner, "the good news is today in America, young people are the most accepting and tolerant people in the history of our nation. We have more good meaning, loving kids in college than ever before. Kids that don't care if you're Black, gay, Jewish, Muslim, or purple. The future is bright despite the deep societal racism. Let's not lose sight of that."

I'll try to remember that, Dr. West, the next time someone shits on me because I'm Jewish. Oh wait, that was just last Tuesday. In the year 2020, if you were wondering. Now imagine how bad Black folks get it.

Rona Day 78: Republicans Are Immune from Rona

We decided to take a weekend trip to Colorado Springs. Low key. Relaxation. Maybe a hike. Some working out. Takeout from the organic Ethiopian place there. Some writing.

I knew Colorado Springs was on the more conservative side, but I didn't fully realize that meant a rejection of science. In the past, Republican didn't mean "anti-science." But lately you see people from Orange County, California to upstate New York screaming at Walmart workers for enforcing simple mask requirements.

The first hint of what was to be in Colorado Springs was when I stopped for gas two miles outside the city. Not one person was wearing a mask. Not the people behind the counter.

Not the customers. I was hoping these few people were the exception.

Not so fast.

We had to stop at Walgreens because my stressed Jewish stomach often needs Nexium, and I forgot to bring my stash from home. I figured at least the people at Walgreens would take precautions. But even there, the cashier and the dozen or so customers were lollygagging like the pandemic was one big hoax. No masks. No distancing. Not even extra bottles of hand sanitizer around. It felt like a Trump rally.

The only people wearing masks at Cheyenne Mountain Resort where we were staying were the three nuclear Black families we noticed, all responsible, which brings me to the topic of stereotyping.

Father's Day is tomorrow, and I can't tell you how many times my Black male friends get an "atta boy" from white co-workers or friends for being good fathers. "I'm so glad you stuck with it," my friend Dwayne's white neighbor proudly told him on Father's Day in 2019. My Black friend Joe hears the same thing at least a dozen times a year. "Good for you not abandoning your kids," was the last "compliment."

Stuck with it? Good for you not abandoning your kids? What? Black men can't be good fathers? Nobody ever congratulated me for not abandoning my kids.

Of course, there are higher rates of single parent households in the Black community. That's common for every community inflicted with higher rates of poverty, stress, lack of opportunity, and crime. But there's nothing about being a person of color that has anything to do with parenthood. Actually, to the contrary, Black men who have opportunities and education typically work extra hard to end the cycle of poverty and trauma inflicted by this nation. I stand in awe of how wonderful so many Black fathers are to their kids. Friends like Ryan. Eric. Mario. Rick. Joe. Dwayne. Charles. Jevard. Matt. David. Dean. Joshua. Durrell. Billy.

The list is much longer. And I have much to learn from each of them.

Rona Day 79: Father's Day

The Lifetime channel, known for their unending movies about abusive men and tormented women, decided to have a "bad dads" movie marathon today. If it was Comedy Central, I might've understood the thought process behind that decision. But really? Bad dads?

Nasty dads aside, I love being a father. It's great to raise thoughtful, woke, fun, and happy kids, but it's even more significant how much I learn from them. Since their births, each has been their own high-powered microscope, with me as the specimen, while they digest my every move and word. If I'm being completely truthful, they're the reason I strive to be a far better person than I was before they entered this world. How they act as adults is going to reflect more on what I did than what I ever told them to do.

It's why when you tell kids not to be racist but then never invite Black families into your home, the kids can still grow up with unconscious racism and bias. Stop telling your kids not to be racist. Just don't act like one. It's bad enough when the walls are painted white. Don't make all the people sitting at your chairs that way too.

Rona Day 80

I scanned through my social media feeds yesterday and not once did someone post "All Parents Matter."

Same thing happened last October during Breast Cancer Awareness month. Not one "All Diseases Matter" response to the awful disease that inflicts so many women.

I'm going to go out on a limb. On July Fourth this year, I'm guessing nobody at any ill-advised COVID Trump rallies will proclaim that All Nations Matter.

Rona Day 81: Racial Distancing

There's a lot of talk about what the new normal will be like after we emerge from this Corona mess. Work from home more. Fridays off. Washing hands more. Maybe even recycle or ride our bikes more to be eco conscious. Support local businesses. Spend more time with kids.

And now, after racial issues finally are center in our minds, let's talk about what the new racial normal will be. Until George Floyd and the ensuing protests and riots, most people weren't even talking about race. Maybe it's because the stores were all closed, so we haven't had as many race-related incidents on the news. Maybe less people were driving so there weren't as many traffic stops, solely for driving while Black while in the "wrong neighborhood." Or maybe it's just because we've always tried to pretend racism either is a thing of the past or isn't all that bad. Or confined to the fringe KKK types.

Until the sixth grade, I only knew one Black kid. James. He was studious, smart, and other than the color of his skin, he was basically the same as the rest of our twenty-six white classmates, plus one Asian kid. James spoke the same way we did. Lived in the same white neighborhood as most of the other classmates. He liked the same cartoon characters. He played on our little league baseball team, although he wasn't that coordinated, so he mostly sat on the bench. None of us kids really thought much about his color. He was just James. Smart, straight-A-student James. He would later go on to be the valedictorian of our high school.

It was 1980 and the big talk in the Columbus public school system was desegregation. I didn't know what this meant at age Eleven, but I overheard my parents discussing how Judge Duncan ordered the schools to develop a program to integrate. They eventually called it busing. Where black and white kids would have to take school buses to different school districts away from their own neighborhoods. The goal was to make the schools a tossed salad of race. So when I showed up for the first day of sixth grade at Yorktown Middle School, I had new bused-in classmates. Lots of them. James was no longer the only kid with darker skin. Half my class was, and they were nothing like James.

Some were smart. Some were dumb. Some spoke with a slang I had only heard the few times I watched the sitcom *Sanford and Son*. Many of the new dark-skinned boys were good at sports. They didn't all like the same cartoons, though. Instead of going to video arcades each weekend, they largely preferred roller-skating rinks. Every Friday night at United Skates of America. I had never even been roller-skating. Most of the kids were from the inner-city neighborhood Olde Towne where my mom taught fifth grade. Boarded up homes. Occasional loud stereo systems blasting out of early model large American cars with broken mufflers. Oldsmobile Cutlass Supremes. Chevy Novas. Always a few people just walking around the streets smoking cigarettes. At least that's what I saw the few times Mom took me to her school to help make her bulletin boards before the year began.

The not-so-funny thing is our pothole-infested street wasn't much better. The four blocks of streets surrounding our house on Shenandoah Drive hadn't been repaved in at least two decades. But our neighbors were all white. Lower middle-class laborers. An occasional semitruck Peterbilt cab parked four doors down from our twelve-hundred-square-feet one-car garage house. Cars on blocks, with neighbors sometimes underneath them doing repairs that never seemed to get finished. Lots of Republicans.

We were shunned as the only family with a foreign-made vehicle, with our Caucasian-colored Japanese Datsun 210. Everyone else only bought American. After all, Japan bombed Pearl Harbor. Oh, and lots of American flags. Our neighbor Mr. Edwards actually had a twenty-five-foot flagpole in his front yard like the kind you see outside schools. We were the only Jews on our street. Heck, we were the only Jews I knew who lived in a neighborhood like ours. We were also the lone Democrats.

I wasn't afraid of our new classmates, unlike many of the other white kids. But I was definitely curious. Who were these dark-skinned kids? They were different and I wanted to know why.

"Hey, I'm Jeff. What's your name," I asked the five-foot-nine sixth grader sitting next to me in homeroom the first day of school. Terrence's skin was way darker than James's. "Terrence, but my teammates call me Big T," he responded with a wide smile. Over the next six months of homeroom, Big T and I talked about everything eleven-year-olds talked about. Television. Sports. Girls. Our families. Music. More girls. But I watched *Superman* and *Wide World of Sports*. He watched *Fat Albert* and the Harlem Globetrotters. I had listened to the Eagles and The Cars. He was listening to Michael Jackson and New Edition. I enjoyed *Andy Griffith* and *Happy Days*, while he was busy laughing hysterically at *Good Times* and

The Jeffersons. I played baseball. He played basketball. He knew how to dance. I could barely do the bunny hop. And on and on it went. I had no idea there was an alternate universe just a forced bus ride away. The other new kids I met, Leonard, Talia, Sharice, Theo, and Ben to name a few, pretty much liked the same things as Terrence. Sure, they all had their own unique flavors, but the Black kids lived in a world I was only now discovering.

It wasn't just new music or different television shows, though. There was something about these kids that was fundamentally different. They had a deeper laugh. The way they hugged and greeted each other. How they smiled. The way they clasped hands in a you're-really-my-brother kind of way. The comfortable and relaxed way they spoke to each other. A camaraderie among them that I had never seen before. I knew they had something the rest of us didn't, and I wanted in on the secret. I devoured every morsel of education from my new friends and remained in awe of their world.

Fast forward thirty plus years and that busing experiment catapulted society into an integrated workforce. Black and white laborers working side by side. In factories. On construction sites. In restaurants. Professionals, too. In law firms. Banks. Advertising agencies. So you'd think that once we got to know each other, we'd all just connect like I did in middle school. The problem, though, is we never integrated after five p.m. in this country. For the most part, Black folks return to their neighborhoods. White folks return to theirs. Virtually nobody spends time in each other's homes.

Reminds me when I was on a panel with Dr. Cornel West back in 2018. We were discussing race issues in front of over a hundred wealthy, mostly white male CEOs. At the end, there was a question and answer session and one CEO of a tech company, his personal worth over one hundred million, asked this in the most genuine tone: "What can I tell my kids so they are less racist than we are?"

I paused. Contemplating his use of the phrase "less racist," even though he didn't mean the way it actually sounds.

"Well, first, our goal isn't to be less racist. It's to not be racist," I started with a smile, half reprimanding him and half letting him know I knew he didn't mean it that way.

"Here's the thing," I continued. "You can't tell your kids to not be racist. If you tell your kids be honest be honest be honest, and then one day at AMC movie theaters you tell the teenager selling you tickets that your daughter is eleven so you can save an extra dollar fifty on the movie when really she's twelve, you just undid all those be honests. In fact, you taught your kid that you can lie even to save a dollar fifty on a *Frozen 2* movie ticket.

It's the same with race. Telling your kids don't be racist. Don't be racist. Don't be racist. But then in your house, only white folks are ever at your dinner table. You've essentially taught your kids that it's okay to keep Black folks separate. At a distance. To treat them as less. Not welcome in your home. Not part of regular society."

I had hit a chord as the millionaire audience went guilty silent.

Even places where some Blacks live among many whites, a friendly hello every time your neighbor Alfred walks outside to water his lawn isn't enough. When did you have Alfred and his family over for dinner, or to family functions? A smile isn't enough. A hello isn't enough.

When we create our new normal, how about we integrate our homes with more colors. Maybe then we can put an end to racial distancing. And an end to systemic racism, backed by our collective unconscious bias.

Rona Day 82: Read!

When I moved to St. Louis in 1995, I shouldn't have been, but I was shocked that one of the main streets there was named Lindbergh. After famed aviator and World Wildlife Fund advocate Charles Lindbergh. You know, that American hero who flew solo nonstop from New York to Paris. But there was another part of Mr. Lindbergh that conveniently goes unnoticed.

Good ole Lucky Lindy was a Nazi sympathizer during World War II and the unofficial spokesperson for America First, which vigorously advocated that the U.S. not fight Jew-massacring Adolph Hitler. Lindbergh regularly gave rousing speeches to crowds of thousands, which included many Nazi supporters. American hero? Not to me. It irritates me to no end that we not only forgot his bigoted ideas, like we have with other bigots such as Henry Ford and Walt Disney, but we actually name streets after these people.

These days, lots of furious protestors have been knocking down statues of Confederate generals and other leaders who not only owned slaves but fought to preserve the entire system of slavery. Slavery. You know that system of mass abuse, rape, labor and the like. People trying to tear down statues of Andrew Jackson, who brutally massacred Native Americans. College football stars now refuse to play in Mississippi so long as it keeps its version of the Confederate flag.

I know what's really bugging you naysayers who argue that these statues are a part of history and should remain. You're afraid you'll have to start reading books. The ten-minute visit to your county courthouse to celebrate the generals who fought against and lost to Abraham Lincoln's United States military will no longer be enough education.

Why don't we preserve our nation's disturbing history in books and museums that chronicle the disturbing events? Kind of like they do in Germany. Last time I checked, there were no statues of famed Nazi generals or labor camp managers there.

And while you're at it, could you finally rename Lindbergh Boulevard to something more palatable, like Fuck Hitler Avenue?

Rona Day 84

So many people are screaming scared that police forces will be defunded or disbanded. Must feel pretty awful to think that their lives may be disrupted by crime at some point.

Now back to solving not just your problems, but others' too.

Rona Day 85

Decided to do some writing today at a coffee shop in Denver, Whittier Café. It's been a great way to help support a Black-owned business and I've already met some dynamic people writing outside on their patio for the last few weeks, tables distanced of course. The patio usually is a Neapolitan selection of activists, writers, grad students and the like. The overheard conversations are quite often about fixing society. The vibe is good. The learning is even better. Latinix, Ethiopians, Black Lives Matter members, professors, you name it.

The bathroom there even has a display of political signs behind the sink:

What's easier to buy than a gun? A POLITICIAN!
CARE LESS ABOUT THIGH GAPS AND MORE ABOUT WAGE GAPS
I'm MARCHING because I know TWEETING won't get me ANYWHERE
JUSTICE FOR BRE
Lessons for ~~my children~~ TRUMP:
1. No bullying ever
2. Tell the truth

3. Limit screen time
4. Use your manners
5. Keep your tiny hands to yourself!

Today, though, a twenty-something-year-old woman and her, I guess now former, similar-aged boyfriend got into an argument. He said something quietly and apparently highly offensive, and in response she flung her iced coffee across the table, hitting him square in the chest and spraying another two or three people at the tables over ten feet away. I personally think iced coffee is disgusting, but I'd prefer it that way if I was going to get it tossed at me. It was a direct shot across his chest, to be sure, but also a reminder that even as we hyper-focus on COVID-19 and racism, life still has its normal bumps, challenges, and trauma.

People didn't stop suffering from the rest of life's curveballs and bullshit.

Rona Day 86: Tom Brokaw's Greatest Generation

The amount of people complaining about coronavirus mask requirements climbs each day. "My rights." "My body." "Don't you tell me what to do, Mr. Government!" "How dare you Mr. Walmart greeter tell me I can't come in without a mask!"

Let's take our time machine back to September 16, 1940. World War II in the waiting. President Franklin Roosevelt just signed into law legislation requiring men between the ages of twenty-one and forty-five to sign up for the draft. A draft that would not end until World War II was over. 1946. Ten million people registered. And a total of 405,399 U.S. military personnel dead.

Now let's go to 1950. The Korean War. A total of 217,000 Americans drafted, and 36,574 dead.

Fast forward to 1964. Another 2.2 million men drafted to fight in Vietnam, with 58,209 dead.

Now let's take a ride to the year year, 2020. Wear your mask, avoid large gatherings for a year, stay home with your families more, and social distance. Oh, the sacrifices that are being asked of us! This generation of so much self-sacrifice for the greater good.

Devastating, I tell you.

Rona Day 87: Palestinian Lives Matter

I'm a bit disappointed some Black Lives Matter leaders and followers continue to conflate the dispute between Israel and the Palestinians with racism in the U.S. Today, there were marchers in Washington D.C. that were chanting *Israel murders children* and then the leader recited a disgusting anti-Semitic poem about the Jewish state being the puppet master of the world. An oft repeated "Jews control the world" bullshit theme anti-Semites like Henry Ford and Adolph Hitler repeated umpteen times. Another march in Brooklyn today featured protestors shouting, "Death to Israel!" Something you might hear in Tehran.

Not that Palestinians aren't deserving of their own homeland or that Israelis and Palestinians shouldn't try harder to find an end to occupying them, it's just those issues are so unrelated to racism in the U.S. that it actually delegitimizes and alienates many fighting for a better life for Black folks in America. Set aside that well over over sixty-five percent of Israeli Jews are people of color from North Africa, the Middle East and Spain, the dispute in the Middle East simply isn't about systemic racial issues against people because of their skin color. Anyone who has ever studied the dispute knows that's the case. Anyone who's been there knows it's not a color issue.

My admitted love for Israel dates back to when I was almost five. We lived in a lower-income apartment complex around the block from Leewood Elementary School in Columbus. Two bedrooms. One for Mom and Dad, and one for me and my one year-old baby brother and his hand-me-down wooden crib. You know, the kind that would never pass a safety test today.

It was 1973. October to be exact. I only remember because Mom already started to make my Halloween costume. We didn't have the money to buy one of those expensive plastic Superman ones my neighbor Henry wore. So, using scraps from various clothing, cheap eyeliner, and some art supplies she used in her substitute teaching job, Mom figured out how to make me into a leopard. It was the same for our birthdays in those early years. Instead of paying a baker fifty dollars to create some fancy cake, Mom baked and decorated my cakes from scratch. One year she even made a choo choo train cake, with four different train car–elongated cakes attached to each other.

At the time, I felt the pain of being in a family with no money, but looking back, I was quite blessed to have a mom who no matter what our financial situation, made sure to shower her love on us.

The other thing I remember is that we had a small black and white TV. A thirteen-inch model. RCA was the brand. Today most of us watch television on fifty, sixty, or even now seventy-inch TVs. Back then, thirteen. With an antenna, and some foil Dad attached to one of the antennae to do what he said would help us get a better signal. Every day like clockwork, Mom and Dad would watch the news. CBS. Walter Cronkite. We had just returned from way too many hours at our synagogue, Temple Israel, because it was the holiest Jewish holiday.

Yom Kippur. I fortunately got to play with other kids in the babysitting room while the adults had to sit through three hours of Hebrew songs nobody could understand. My baby brother just slept through the entire thing. Lucky bastard.

"Oh my God! The Arabs attacked Israel. On Yom Kippur. That's the lowest of the low. Damn bastards," I heard Dad tell Mom as Cronkite announced that Arab armies from multiple countries had attacked Israel on the holiest day of the Jewish calendar to catch them off guard while they were praying in synagogue. I had no idea what a bastard was until years later, but that was Dad's go-to political insult for most of my childhood. I always thought it meant "terrorists" and was surprised to learn it was just someone born to parents out of wedlock. "There's no way they'll beat Israel," Dad continued. "Israel has the best military in the world."

Israel was so central to our childhood that years later, when I was eighteen and sneaking through an old box of Swisher Sweets cigars my Grandpa had saved and filled with random junk, I stumbled upon an Israel bond from October 1973. The month and year Israel was attacked. Despite our having no money, Dad bought an Israel bond at $175 face value. The best part is that he bought it in my name. When I turned eighteen, I could cash it in, which I promptly did then. That was a lot of money to me back in 1987.

As a kid, everything we were taught about Israel was fantastic and amazing. By the time I was seven, I knew that Israel was the only democracy in the Middle East. I knew that it produced more science and inventions than the entire rest of the Arab world combined. The nation was 1/667th the size but one thousand times the output. I learned that women could even be prime minister in Israel. I knew that Israel had a thriving ecological and environmental program. That it turned a dessert into an oasis. Israel even helped farmers in Africa learn how to work the land.

In later years, I would go on to learn about Israel's cures for multiple cancers, its groundbreaking research for MS, its invention of the cell phone, and numerous microchips used in computers. A space program. IsraAID, which sends teams of experts to places like Haiti and Turkey when natural disasters strike. I knew gay people had rights in Israel. I knew it had Nobel Prize winners in a dozen or so categories. More startup companies than almost any country, save the U.S. and Japan. Israel, the size of New Jersey, was a beacon of hope and accomplishment. The perfect country.

Even more, I knew Israel had done all that while surrounded by numerous countries dedicated to their destruction. Who had attacked them for decades. Lebanon and Hezbollah. Hamas. Syria. Egypt. Jordan. Saudi Arabia. Libya. All had tried to take Israel out at one time or another. Suicide bombings. Plane hijackings. Armed PLO members throwing Israeli kids from classrooms. Israeli athletes killed at the Munich Olympics. The entire Arab world at Israel's throat. But none of it seemed to stop Israel from climbing the ladder of nations. I was proud of my spiritual homeland. The place Jews had been exiled from but never lost their hope to return. For those who deny that connection, simply visit. The thousands of years of Jewish history stares you in the face almost everywhere you go.

As an adult, I've traveled to Israel several times to see firsthand Israel's greatness. In recent years, I've visited desalination plants that turn ocean water into drinking water. I've witnessed how Israel recycles all of its wastewater and uses it for farming. Yes, I've tasted what I called a poop-grown strawberry. I've seen how Israel's cutting-edge drip irrigation technology has revolutionized farming in the U.S. in areas where water is scarce.

I've visited startup incubators where Israelis are solving some of the world's most devasting issues. I drank clean water from a machine that removes water from the air even in dry climates. I visited medical research labs that are working hard to stem the tide of Alzheimer's and dementia. Multiple sclerosis breakthroughs. New drug therapies to beat some of the worst cancers.

I've even visited hospitals where Israeli doctors have saved Palestinian and other Arab lives in surgery not available in most of the Arab world. One facility where Israeli soldiers snuck in Arabs who were wounded in the civil war in Syria and provided medical care.

Still, with all that greatness, as an adult I've also had to learn the hard truth for me that Israel is far, far, far from the perfect nation I was once taught. I've been to Palestinian communities completely cut off from family members by concrete barriers erected by Israel. I've visited areas where Palestinian farmers were forced to move so Israel could build more apartments for its fast-growing communities in the West Bank. Israel has confiscated more and more land and moved more Israelis into areas that by any standard would have been part of an independent Palestinian country.

I've watched with tears videos of Israeli soldiers beating Palestinians, already restrained and no longer a threat. I've listened to some Israelis on the streets speak of their Palestinian neighbors as if they were animals. I heard firsthand how my own peaceful unarmed uncle, nonviolent and seventy-six years old, was pushed to the ground by a twenty-year-old Israeli solider for protesting Israeli encroachment on Palestinian land. I've read the eye-witness accounts by Israeli writers on some of the abuse

Israeli soldiers too often inflict on Palestinians. I recall in 2014 the Palestinian fifteen-year-old from Tampa, Florida who was brutally beaten by Israeli soldiers. Tariq Khdeir. Say his name.

I'm not foolish or naïve enough to think that Israel doesn't oftentimes face real dangers. Nor am I self-hating to somehow compare Israel to numerous places committing far worse crimes. Still, my standard for the Jewish homeland was and has never been, "We're better than Iran or North Korea." My bar is not "Well, in Russia, they imprison gays and arrest dissenters."

Let's be clear. The Palestinians don't have a country of their own. A place where they do not have to travel through Israeli checkpoints and get searched to go from one city to another. Where they don't have to see Israeli soldiers enter their cities. Where they can farm their land without fear Israel will take it away. Where they get a seat at the table of nations. Palestinians also have a strong emotional and national connection to the land loved by Jews.

Most Jews boastfully point out that Israel has offered peaceful solutions numerous times which would have resulted in a Palestinian state. Each time for over fifty years, the Palestinians have refused because they didn't get everything they wanted. Each time they reject the plan. Even Bill Clinton was shocked that Yasser Arafat, Chairman of the Palestinian Liberation Organization and leader of the Palestinian people, turned down a comprehensive offer to put the dispute to rest.

It's true; Israel has in the past made many offers. But it's also true that right-wing Palestinians and Israeli war hawks owe their very existence and power to the dispute. Without it they become irrelevant.

Still, these peace efforts aren't excuses for Israel to continue seizing land, building settlements, and roughhousing

Palestinians. These aren't excuses for Palestinians, particularly in Gaza, to build tunnels into Israel and attack Israeli schools. Or to shoot rockets at Israeli hospitals. These just give each side more and more reason *not* to resolve the conflict.

I've been to Jericho. I've been to several Palestinian villages. I've been to Ramallah. I've met Palestinian farmers. I've spoken with Palestinian National Authority security officers. I've visited Arab communities in Egypt and Jordan. I've sat with Palestinian peace advocates. I also know many Palestinians and other Arabs here in the U.S.

Similarly, I've spent time on Israeli military bases. I've talked to Israeli generals and security officials and politicians. I've spent time along the Israeli-Egyptian border, the Israeli-Lebanese border, and the Israeli-Syrian border. I've met with and talked to everyday Israelis. Farmers. Bus drivers. People in Tel Aviv. Jerusalem. The Golan. The border and often bombed community of Sderot.

While there are certainly Palestinians who are dangerous and some who are terrorists, and while there are certainly aggressive Israelis who serve with weapons in the country's military and security forces who often collide with Palestinians, the vast majority of Israelis and Arabs care about the same things. They want their kids to get a good education. They want jobs. They want health and wellness. And most of all, religious extremists and nationalists aside, they both want peace among neighbors.

I am pro-Israel. I am pro-Palestinian. But I'm not okay with the loud few on the far left here at home abusing the cause for civil rights and equity in the U.S. by melting the Israeli-Palestinian conflict into their platform. The issues in the Middle East are not the same as our slavery, Jim Crow, and mass incarceration. The issues in the Middle East are not based on skin color. They have their own unique complexities centered around two peoples loving the same land.

Still, as a very close young Saudi friend of mine so aptly pointed out recently, if Israel can be a light to the world in microchips, medicine, automated cars, the environment, and a whole host of other cutting-edge creations, it can certainly use its creative minds to solve the Palestinian conflict.

Rona Day 88: July Fourth

Remember on this U.S. Independence Day to shout it loud like I know you do every year:

ALL NATIONS MATTER

Rona Day 89

The administration has done it again. New rules came out today telling foreign students that they must leave the country if their university has mostly online courses this fall because of COVID-19. Message to young Chinese, Saudis, Indians, and Mexicans: Either risk your life going to classes or get the fuck out of our country. Either way, your life doesn't matter here in the land of the not-quite-free and home of the not-so-brave.

On some issues, I can see why well-intentioned people tried early on to make excuses for the president. "We need to stop people from illegally entering the country." "We need to vet people so we don't let in terrorists." "We can't just have open borders." None of these in a vacuum is offensive. Most of us agree with those principles.

But Trump seems motivated by something other than smart immigration policies. Even when policies are bad for the U.S. economically, Trump stands by his anti-immigration and anti–people of color rules and speeches.

Take his reduction of immigration numbers. Farmers and technology companies alike will tell you that we simply do not have enough people in the U.S. with the skills or desire to perform much needed work. Students attending schools contribute billions to the economy (forty-five billion, to be exact) each year. Some stay, some do not. But either way, they are here renting apartments, buying cars, eating at our restaurants, adding to our diverse discussions in schools. Whether they help the U.S. excel or their home countries prosper, they will contribute to the success of the world one way or another.

Makes you wonder what motivates this president. Would anyone have even thought of promulgating these rules if our international students came from England, Ireland, or Norway?

Rona Day 90

Lots of people claiming the only reason we have more Corona cases is because we have more testing. Not sure that explains the surge in hospitalizations, but I was thinking maybe we could also increase IQ testing while we're at it.

Rona Day 91

Today NFL wide receiver DeSean Jackson decided it was a good idea to post horrifically anti-Semitic quotes by Adolph Hitler and Louis Farrakhan. He took the first set down, then reposted what he thought was a watered-down version. Still anti-Semitic though. The age-old *Jews control the world* crap.

I can deal with anti-Semites. Whatever color they come in. In fact, I prefer my haters to be open and honest about their disdain for certain groups of people. What I don't do well with is silence in response to hate.

The NFL and its players have largely remained completely silent over Jackson's tirade against Jews. The same people who were quite loud when Drew Brees was rightfully put in his place after he chose George Floyd's death as a good time to talk about not disrespecting our flag by taking a knee.

Set aside that Hitler didn't even make the statement quoted by DeSean Jackson, which suggested that Black people are the "real Jews" and today's Jews are imposters (an oft repeated historical lie by Farrakhan)—the fact that anyone thinks it's okay to quote Hitler or other anti-Semites with the absurd notion Jews control the world is disgusting.

If we are to change systems of racism, we must be consistent in our intolerance for all kinds of hate. I thought we were telling cops and white folks not to be silent bystanders anymore.

Is that standard not applicable to hate against Jews? Is that how we roll?

Check yourself. Don't be the hate you want to see changed in others.

Rona Day 92: Ethnic Narcissism and DeSean Jackson

I've been thinking a lot these days about why so many people are hesitant to call out their own. Black NFL and other sports players have largely been silent on DeSean Jackson. Silent on Farrakhan. Silent on Black Lives Matter folks who falsely accuse Israel of genocide.

I think I finally figured it out. I call it ethnic narcissism.

Let me first take you to Trump Heights, Israel. How does that feel when it rolls off your tongue? That's the name of a new community in the Golan Heights, in northern Israel along the Syrian border. Prime Minister Netanyahu unveiled the new town at a naming ceremony last year, touting Trump as a great friend of Israel. This, right after Trump recognized Israel's sovereignty over the Golan Heights, which was captured in 1967 after defeating Syria in one of Israel's many wars.

While the government of Israel still has not earmarked any money to actually create the city offensively named to so many people worldwide, myself included, and though many see the move as another one of Netanyahu's frequent publicity stunts, the fact is that the touted only democracy in the Middle East is clinging to one of America's most divisive, mean, and race-baiting presidents since Richard Nixon.

This was nothing compared to how embarrassed I was as a Jew to watch my co-religionists give Trump a standing ovation at an AIPAC conference a few years ago. I'd been to past AIPAC conferences and they typically were filled with politicians of both parties there to do nothing more than support the elected government of Israel, left or right, but I can't recall ever witnessing standing ovations for such divisive figures. I stopped attending the conferences years ago as my dislike for Netanyahu increased.

To be fair, Trump has been one of Israel's most vocal supporters ever. He recognized Jerusalem as the official capital of the Jewish homeland instead of just promising to do so like the past five presidents before him. He and Ambassador Nikki Haley finally put their foot down at the United Nations where Israel was regularly and unfairly vilified as a human rights violator while places like Iran, North Korea, Russia, China, and other abusive regimes got far less or almost no criticism despite doing far worse. While gay pride parades were taking place in Israel, and Russia was busy jailing its gays, the UN was trouncing Israel. Not a peep about Russia.

Trump has even refused to fund international organizations that unfairly target Israel above countries leading the world in abuse. I'll set aside whether carte blanche support for Netanyahu is truly good for Israel, or actually helps foster lasting peace with our valuable Palestinian cousins, but the optics are that Trump always takes Israel's side.

We ought not overstate things. Most Jews in the U.S. disapprove of Trump despite his outward unwavering support for Israel. Still, there's enough of us who let Trump slide on his barrage of bigotry and anti-immigrant statements and policies, even though Jews have been largely at the forefront of the other side of those issues, all in the name of "he's good for Israel" and "he's good for the Jews."

Still, why would Jews, the Jews who marched with Dr. King and the Jews who were lynched for protesting Black inequality in the South, clap for Trump? Why would the Jewish homeland, which like it or not represents Jews worldwide, name a city after a man who by no measure follows any of our Jewish values?

Why would some Jews even favor Netanyahu at this point, who really is just a smarter and more polished version of our bombastic president?

The answer is simple. Because we Jews love ourselves. A lot.

In a world that has massacred us. Gassed us. Starved us. Experimented on us. Forced conversion on us. Exiled us. Beat us. Enslaved us. Jailed us. Murdered our kids. Someone finally is speaking up for us other than fellow Jews. Trump speaks up for the Jewish homeland. And it feels good. How dare anyone else tell us we now have to distance ourselves from, or criticize, one of the few people who stands up for our spiritual homeland.

It's nothing less than ethnic narcissism. Where one's love for their own group overshadows all other important values.

Now calm down my fellow Jews. Every abused or marginalized group has this disease. We aren't the only ones.

A good friend of mine, who was an alderman in St. Louis years ago, decided to attend the Million Man March, led by none other than Hitler-praising Louis Farrakhan. The same man who's called Judaism a "dirty religion" and called Jews "termites." Whose *Final Call* publication has blamed Jews for the World Trade Center bombing and Kennedy's assassination. Who published a book falsely and downright absurdly blaming the entire slave trade on Jews. Who's called today's Jews imposters. A man who literally has dedicated a good chunk of his life to defaming Jews. Even his July 4, 2020 address continued his barrage against Jews. Where do you think wide receiver De-Sean Jackson got his motivation to tweet out anti-Jew garbage?

I remember my twenty-something-year-old self being furious at my brown-skinned friend for attending the Farrakhan march in D.C. How could a loving person like my friend. A politician I supported. A person who regularly fights for justice. A person who has many Jewish friends and supporters. How could he of all people attend an event hosted by such an avowed anti-Semite? It hurt our friendship at the time.

The same holds true for the now revered Malcolm X. People wear his shirts and boast his greatness. Schools and streets are named after him. All despite Malcolm's many vicious anti-Semitic statements. Even some Black Lives Matter leaders falsely accuse Israel of genocide, ignoring that the Palestinian population has skyrocketed over five hundred percent during this alleged genocidal massacre.

We Jews pounce on people who support these anti-Semites. We chew on them and spit them out. We shout it from the rooftops. We live by the post-Holocaust slogan NEVER AGAIN will we ever be silent toward hate against our people. It's why Jews need Israel. Some place to make sure the world never comes close to wiping us out again.

When Jesse Jackson defamed us. When Reverend Al Sharpton defamed us. We pounced on them. Rightfully so. They were peddling in the worst kind of millennia-old hate. The Jews as the world puppet masters. Or in Jesse's derogatory word, "hymies."

If you ask some Jews to explain how they can so swiftly criticize Eagles wide-receiver DeSean Jackson for simply repeating what he learned from Farrakhan, yet simultaneously give standing ovations and atta-boys to Donald Trump, you'll likely get a "how can you compare the two?" You'll get a long list of Trump's support for Israel. And you'll get a complete whitewashing and excuse list to explain away Trump's attitudes and statements about people of color, Africa, immigrants, and Muslims.

For Black people who listen to and support the Farrakhans, anti-Israel BLM leaders, and Jesse Jacksons of the world, you'll get a virtually identical response. "I don't listen to the side show. I don't pay attention to the anti-Jew stuff. I'm listening because they speak about Black empowerment. About Black self-determination. About Black economics. About ending racism against Blacks."

You see, every marginalized or abused group takes whatever support they can get, because in their world, they daily have to deal with, in the case of Black folks, mass systemic racism, police abuse, housing racism, financial racism, environmental racism, etc., etc., etc. Their leaders have been shot and maimed. Investigated by the FBI, which once called Dr. King one of the most dangerous threats to the U.S. Their leaders are discredited and put down. Even a quarterback nonviolently taking a knee to end police abuse is called antimilitary. Anti-American. Nobody raising any eyebrows is okay in the eyes of many white folks. The deep hatred against the classy and even-keeled President Obama was so far beyond the pale, it's hard to imagine it was for any other reason than race for many.

So when a leader stands up. Finally. To fight for Black folks. It's not about their side shows, however offensive. It's about their pro-Black action. It's about someone. Anyone. Finally standing up to oppression. And not giving a fuck who likes it or not.

Makes you think maybe some of y'all should have better appreciated the numerous righteous Black leaders you criticized, shot, lynched, or sent to the dustbins of history.

Make no mistake. Recent research polling of Black attitudes toward Jews and Israel, despite only one in three Blacks having a Jewish friend in the U.S., shows that only ten percent of Black people actually have negative or very negative views of the Jewish state. An astounding seventy percent of Black people sympathize equally with Israel and the Palestinians, with a majority supporting Israel's security as a nation. Close to sixty percent of Black people say their feelings are based on the fact that Jews have also suffered oppression.

Half understand that Dr. King was a strong supporter of the Jewish people (forty percent weren't sure). Close to half know that Jews were instrumental to the civil rights movement. A solid majority believe Israel lives in a dangerous neighborhood. And over sixty percent of African Americans believe that the Jewish homeland is an eternal promise of God to Abraham. While there are some negative attitudes by lower percentages of Black people against Jews, the overwhelming number of Black people don't hate Jews. In fact, positive views are common.

Numerous Black leaders from W.E.B. Du Bois to Martin Luther King, Jr. to Medgar Evers to Corey Booker to numerous pastors in churches across America for decades stood and still stand with Jews. At one of our own Denver MLK celebrations in 2020, speech after speech from Black pastors proclaimed their solidarity with the Jewish people.

Like Black folks, when someone finally stands up for Jews, and Jews clap, it's not because of the bigoted side shows. However nasty or racist. It's about their pro-Jewish action.

Attitudes of Jews toward Black people are way more empathetic in national poll after national poll than all other ethnic groups in the U.S. Every single one. Jews in high numbers believe it's their moral obligation to stand up for Black people. Jewish organizations invest time and money in fighting racism and even file civil rights lawsuits. I'll leave for another time whether left-wing politics helps Black people or not, but Jews vote Democrat consistently near eighty percent. That's higher than any other ethnic group besides Black people. Jews were instrumental in founding the NAACP and Urban League. I could go on. I've been in numerous board meetings and Jews, even behind closed doors, are always talking about equality and figuring out how they can help. It's part of our psyche.

It's understandable on some level that abused and oppressed groups are hyper-focused on stomping out the hate they endure. It's understandable why these groups cling to anyone who will champion their causes. Often at the expense of others.

But, until we achieve the higher level where hate against any group is intolerable, and not just hate against our own, we will sadly continue to prop up people giving out mind poison like candy. And like it or not, that mind poison is all the reason our detractors need to continue our systems of marginalization and abuse.

Rise above it.
"If I am not for myself, who will be for me?
But if I am only for myself, who am I?
If not now, when?"

—*Mishnah, Ethics of the Fathers*, 1:14,
Rabbi Hillel, First Century

Rona Day 93

It dawned on me this morning how much our simultaneous pandemics, Corona and racism, have in common: People have trouble believing they exist if they haven't been personally affected.

Rona Day 94: The Washington Foreskins

The Washington Redskins announced today that they're getting rid of their eighty-eight-year-old racist name.

I always wondered how people would feel if we had sports teams like the Cleveland Black Faces. Or the Baltimore Jews. Or the New York Gays. The Philadelphia Shiites.

I think we've become so numb to the Redskins name it never dawned on us how offensive that might be to some. But alas, Native Americans aren't mascots. They're human beings.

Unlike, of course, the Notre Dame Fighting Irish. A lot easier to digest when your group isn't already marginalized, isn't it?

Rumor has it *The Redwolves* will be the replacement name. I suppose that's better than the Washington Foreskins. Not exactly what I'd call a cutting-edge name. That might piss off the Sandra Bullocks of the world anyway since she announced on *Ellen* in 2018 that she gets cloned foreskin injections in her face. Ewww. What a dickhead.

Rona Day 95

Quite amazing to me how so many white folks are increasingly angry at hatred coming from Black folks. Lots of buzz on social media feeds about Black hatred against whites.

Oh, the irony.

It was just a few weeks ago when President Trump quoted in a tweet a supposed leader of an unofficial offshoot of BLM stating that "if the U.S. doesn't give us what we want, we will burn down the system and replace it." Forget that the person is not affiliated with BLM and has been criticized by BLM, some white people like to pick out whatever anger they can coming from Black folks to demonstrate their narrative of how hateful Black people are toward whites. Or the repeating of cop-killing slogans chanted by some fringe groups. Or the news showing groups of thirty people in Brooklyn shouting "death to America." Or a small group of fifty yelling anti-white slogans in California.

Set aside that most Black people, despite centuries of abuse, aren't burning us down, or advocating killing or disbanding cops, or hating us all. If you're going to get all heated about hatred, start with the hate that hate creates. Reminds me of the movie, *The Hate U Give*. Acronym, THUG.

Slow down folks. If you don't like poisonous plants to grow, stop watering them.

Rona Day 96: What's in a Name?

It sure would suck to have the name Karen these days. I actually know a Black woman named Karen. Wonder if she's having an identity crisis right now. Once perfectly acceptable, Karen is now defined as a white woman, probably with short hair, complaining about unsuspecting Black people. To managers. To the police. Anyone who will listen. Karen has been relegated to the world of memes. At least for now.

I always thought of Karen as a white girl's name anyway, just like Emily, Madison, Ellen, Amy, Annie, Christy, Molly, and Heidi.

Still, it must feel like having the name Monica during the Bill Clinton affair with Monica Lewinsky. Or Katrina after the hurricane destroyed New Orleans. Or Chucky when the horror movie *Child's Play* came out. It would've sucked having the name Roxanne, when the rock group The Police released their '80s hit. Probably still sucks since the song is still played and has even turned into rap songs. I have a friend Mario, and I'm pretty sure he's glad the Nintendo Mario craze has subsided. I know a few Black girls named Sienna and I'd be willing to bet they're not happy Toyota decided to name a minivan with that name. A sports car, maybe. But a mom-mobile?

Kind of surprised Peter and Dick never went by the wayside. I'm just glad my parents didn't name me Jack. Jack Kass. God, that would've sucked. It's bad enough Dad wanted my first name to be Harold. Mom said "hell no! I'm not having a kid named Harry Kass." Anyway, Harold still ended up my middle name.

Other names were ruined far worse than Karen or Monica. Adolph was pretty much destroyed as a name. Hannibal also isn't so popular these days. Guessing Elsa or Alexa won't be in the baby name winners over the next decade plus. Isis certainly won't be on any birth certificates any time soon. And unless you want your daughter to grow up to be a stripper, Nevaeh is probably out for good.

I suspect Donald will follow these names into the dustbin of history as well. We can only hope.

Rona Day 97

Walmart is now requiring shoppers to wear masks.

Admittedly, I'm not a big Walmart fan. Years ago, it was just because I didn't like how they treated their workers and how they pretty much decimated small-town businesses nationwide. I once read a study that Walmart actually destroyed more jobs than it created. No idea if that's true, but that certainly would add to my disdain for them.

I'm not gonna lie, though, I've always been thoroughly entertained with the pictures going around the internet called "The People of Walmart." Google it. People wearing everything from swimsuits to adult onesies as they shop at Walmart.

The last time I went to Walmart was actually just two weeks ago. I came up with a silly game. My daughter, girlfriend and I each had twenty dollars and twenty minutes. I was tasked with spending up to twenty dollars in gifts for my girlfriend. Naomi had to buy for me. Etc. Each of us had twenty minutes to complete the task. Masks on with distancing of course. I almost ran out of time when I stopped to watch a man sitting in very very short jean shorts and a tank top in the middle of the store, snacking on Kit Kats, wrappers all around him.

The few other times I've been, I witnessed my fair share of other interestingly dressed shoppers. One woman in St. Louis, at the store on Hanley Road, was wearing a halter top with pajama pants with little Tabasco sauce bottles printed all over the pants. I discreetly snapped a picture. Another man I saw had on a light blue hospital gown, and nothing but underpants behind the curtain. Tighty whities, to be specific. The worst, though, was a four-hundred-pound man wearing cargo shorts and no shirt. Belly hanging way over his belt. His poor, poor belt. I didn't stay to watch him bend down to grab a pack of gum off the bottom shelf.

So Walmart, while you're instituting new rules about droplet-preventing mouth and nose coverings, how about requiring visitors to get out of their pajamas and get dressed before buying their next Terra & Sky outfit.

Rona Day 98

While a few Trump supporters I know think COVID-19 is going away November 4, right after the election, one thing is definitely true. Joe Biden's staying in his basement quarantined from interacting with the rest of the world is probably his best chance of winning.

I've become numb to party politics. Both parties have taken their turns running the country for a long time and neither seems to address the deep problems facing so many people. Whether it's income disparity or racial justice, we've got one party which doesn't acknowledge the depth of the problems and the other party which acknowledges them but then tries the same ole stale solutions to address them. Band-Aids, if you will.

In our instant gratification, tweeting, social media feed, TikTok, "Google it" society, we've become far too focused on right this second rather than having the foresight to think globally or about any long-term fixes. If only people could see that we're all on the same ship and there's a bomb on board, set to go off not now but later. Right now, we have the time and resources to build a new boat and get off the boat destined to explode.

If Jeff Bezos, for example, could see that if he sacrificed just a portion of his $300 million *per day* earnings to provide his day-to-day workers, drivers, and those on the warehouse floor, with a far more livable wage, child care, an opportunity for stock ownership and company-sponsored education advancement, those workers would be key in our country's success. The amount they will buy. The manner in which they will be able to care for and educate their kids.

Bezos, born just five years and one day before me, is worth $182 billion and counting. Sadly, I'm not worth anything close to that, yet, so make sure you tell your friends to buy this book. Imagine what his life would be like if he was only worth fifty billion and counting. FIFTY BILLION! No homes sacrificed. No boats he'll have to unload. No Gucci shoes returned. No servants or drivers fired. Nothing would have to be sacrificed. Yet he literally could change the lives of his 840,000 employees, and better the United States in the process.

Rona Day 99: #JewishPrivilege

Lots of Jews have been using the hashtag #JewishPrivilege this past week to sarcastically respond to the joys of being constantly blamed for everything. Lately, it's been Black celebs doing this. DeSean Jackson. Nick Cannon. Ice Cube. Just to name a few.

Of course, hate is sick. It's wrong. It's ugly. And it should be stomped out at every moment.

I don't care if it's a Romanian newspaper, which earlier this year blamed Jews for all of the country's ills. That's right, ten thousand Jews remaining from the many slaughtered by the Romanian-assisted Germans have ruined it for the twenty million other residents.

It doesn't matter if it comes from a Jordanian politician who claimed Jews are related to pigs. Or if its graffiti painted on walls in Venezuela's capital, saying "KILL JEWS" in Spanish. Or if it's from the Malaysian president remarking that "hook-nose Jews rule the world."

Hate is hate is hate is hate.

I don't particularly like the #JewishPrivilege tag, though, because Jews in America, whatever their struggles, look more like the majority white population and have more privileges as a result than people of color who suffer from far deeper systemic racism. No police officer has ever asked my religion when I've been pulled over. No bank loan officer ever asked to see if I was circumcised. We'll set aside my Jewfro for the time being.

But Black folks can't just hide who they are or blend in. They can't simply not tell people their ethnic background. It's on their faces. Duh. So when I hear "Jewish privilege," it feels cheap. We've got people who suffer so deeply as a result of our systems that benefit the many over the few that, to me, it's not the time to distract from the bigger white skin color privilege discussion.

No, I didn't think I was privileged to be Jewish when a swastika was painted on my door in college. Or when white fraternities graffitied Jewish fraternity houses with Nazi crap. Or when I walked to class behind some suburban white kids donning Ralph Lauren shirts listening to them talk about "the fucking brat Jews."

I didn't think it was a privilege when a member of the Nation of Islam tried to grab my neck in law school and screamed "Hitler should've burned all you Jews." I can't even keep those guys straight. One minute the Jews should've been burned, the next minute they claim we aren't even Jewish.

It certainly wasn't a privilege to be Jewish when a white colleague at a law firm made up stories about me so he would become partner first. Especially when I later learned he had made anti-Jewish jokes on a number of occasions. Or when I learned one of my older white male bosses was heard in court, "I'm gonna beat the shit out of that Jew bastard," when referring to the lawyer on the other side of the case.

It wasn't a privilege to have some rednecks scream from their cars "fuck you Jews" when I was walking to synagogue in St. Louis one Saturday morning.

Nor was it a privilege to have a girl in law school tell me "you're cute for a Jew," or another peer exclaim, "I didn't know Jews could dress so well."

It wasn't very privilege-y to have a friend of a friend say, "I'm not a fan of the Jews, but you're cool."

Or to be in a cab in Chicago listening to a white man of Polish descent tell me the Jews exaggerated the Holocaust.

It wasn't a privilege to have someone at dinner at a fancy restaurant laugh to his Jewish girlfriend about how cheap Jews are. Ha, ha.

Nor has it been a privilege to be Jewish knowing how for three thousand years my people have been persecuted everywhere they go. And even now, we're told our homeland is illegitimate all while they don't want us in those same people's countries either.

No wonder I have a weak stomach. It's in the Jewish gene pool.

But my fellow Jewish people, know that the vocal but small number of Black people who defame Jews aren't like the whiteys who butchered us. You see, Black people aren't in any positions of power to do much actual bad to us. I get it. Our feelings are hurt worse when a Black celebrity acts out against us than we are when Donald Trump stereotypes us as nerdy good-with-money accountants. It's probably because we expect the bullshit from white power systems and country clubs who still keep us out. But not from groups who are marginalized. Not from people who also suffer.

I'm not suggesting that Black anti-Semites shouldn't be called out. We ought never to be silent against hate. Period. But we still should place the relative dangers on the side of the right scale. People who hate us in positions of power, like executives at Texaco caught on tape badmouthing Jews years ago. Or politicians like Richard Nixon (whose derogatory recordings about us were quite disturbing). These folks are far more dangerous than a group of marginalized people fighting not to be beat up or killed by cops.

Perspective is something that's been lost by most these days.

Rona Day 100

It's hard to believe we've been at this modified COVID society thing for over a hundred days already. Technically for a bit longer, but it hadn't hit most of us until March. We had all seen it before. SARS. Swine flu. Bird flu. Most of us expected this to just pass like the rest of the scares. We'd been told death and destruction were coming at least five times before.

The thing is, I knew something worse was coming when the Zac Brown concert on March 12 was cancelled. I was scheduled to fly to St. Louis with one of my sons, and just a day before, the cancellation was announced. This wasn't the flu. This wasn't a contained potential threat.

I'm reminded again to count my blessings and to find the good in this chaos. The extra time spent with my teenagers is especially wonderful. The cleaner planet. The fact we've been essentially forced to pay attention to racial distress without our normal distractions. The time for self-reflection on how we can be nicer people when a cure or vaccine is found.

Of course I'm sad for businesses, in particular small businesses which may not recover. I wish our government had done a better job of providing a safety net for such catastrophes, especially since it's quite apparent our response only prolonged the problem. Goldman Sachs announced that had we attacked this virus with masking and distancing in full force back in early March, we would have saved over a trillion dollars in economic damage.

I'm sad for all the people who lost their jobs and keep hanging on by a thread waiting to see if our government will step in to protect them. I was reading statistics the other day of which countries provided free or affordable education. Which ones provided free or affordable health care. Which ones provided safety nets for the most vulnerable. It turns out the U.S. lags behind almost every country in the world in every category, except I think education is more expensive in one country. The leader of the free world isn't leading when it comes to compassion.

I'm not a big fan of free, except for maybe health care. I don't think free jobs, free education, or free housing creates the right mindset for people to achieve and grow. To feel a sense of pride. But our systems are not just not free. They are prohibitively expensive. We ought to have an affordable higher education and vocational system. Affordable housing. Affordable paths to achieve. Right now, we are leaving behind swaths of great families who unnecessarily struggle to make it to tomorrow. COVID only highlighted that disaster.

I'm also sad for people who lost family members too early, even if they were already elderly. Two years shaved off a grandparent's life is still too much.

But let's not forget the oft repeated saying, "this too shall pass." The world has survived pandemics, world wars, starvation, depressions, and natural disasters. We will emerge from these challenging times with hopefully a renewed purpose and focus. One where we commit to making our country and world free for everyone.

About the Author

As an authoritative voice for those committed to the betterment of our world, Jeffrey Kass is a relentless champion for racial and societal engagement. A practicing lawyer, community activist and award-winning author, Jeffrey's insights rattle ingrained thinking, provoke dialogue, and ignite fresh approaches for navigating today's rapidly evolving times.

In addition to this book, Jeffrey also is the author of the *"End Racial Distancing Journal,"* available on Medium.com, as well as the book *"Oreos and a Pack of Marlboro Lights,"* a collection of true traumedy stories. His stories and essays on race, religion, society, the Middle East and politics have appeared in national and regional publications for over twenty five years.

Jeffrey also is a national speaker, and he trains organizations on diversity issues and racism eradication through his unique "End Racial Distancing" method. As a lawyer, he is a partner at the national firm of Lewis Brisbois, where he practices business and intellectual property law.

When he's not writing or lawyering, Jeffrey serves on the executive board of the Urban Leadership Foundation of Colorado, as treasurer of Denver Delta, Inc. (an offshoot foundation board from the black sorority, Delta Sigma Theta) and on the board of the Jewish Community Relations Council of Colorado.

Jeffrey enjoys weightlifting, hiking, playing basketball, reading, cooking gourmet food from around the world, traveling, anything Ohio State, learning languages, cars and fashion.

Above all, he is a proud father of three beautiful teenagers.

You can reach Jeffrey through www.jeffreykassglobal.com

www.ingramcontent.com/pod-product-compliance
Lightning Source LLC
Chambersburg PA
CBHW020019030726
47499CB00007B/2185